BODIES WRAPPED IN PLASTIC

AND OTHER ITEMS OF INTEREST

ANDERSEN PRUNTY

GRINDHOUSE PRESS

BODIES WRAPPED IN PLASTIC

AND OTHER ITEMS OF INTEREST

Also by Andersen Prunty

Deathtripping: Collected Horror Stories
Neon Dies At Dawn
Irrationalia
Failure As a Way of Life
This Town Needs a Monster
Squirm With Me
Creep House: Horror Stories
Sociopaths In Love
The Warm Glow of Happy Homes
Bury the Children in the Yard: Horror Stories
Satanic Summer
Fill the Grand Canyon and Live Forever
Pray You Die Alone: Horror Stories
Sunruined: Horror Stories
The Driver's Guide to Hitting Pedestrians
Hi I'm a Social Disease: Horror Stories
Fuckness
The Sorrow King
Slag Attack
My Fake War
The Beard
Zerostrata
Jack and Mr. Grin
The Overwhelming Urge

BODIES

WRAPPED

IN

PLASTIC

ONE

"You wanna get high and watch *Twin Peaks* later?"

My startled jerk sent the brush I'd been using to clean the toilet into the bathtub next to it. I turned to see the new front desk girl, Marnie O'Dell, standing in the doorway.

I was still trying to find my voice when she said, "Libbie, right?"

I nodded my head.

"Didn't mean to startle you," she said.

"It's . . . it's okay."

"So, you want to?"

I leaned back against the vanity, my legs weak from the adrenaline spike and cleaning rooms all day.

"I mean, it's okay if you don't want to. I just thought . . ." She unbuttoned her shirt, not making eye contact with me. Aside from the dressy blouse, she wore a pair of gray basketball shorts and I wondered if she had worked at the front desk like that or if she'd already swapped out of a skirt or nicer pair of pants. Not that you had to dress up to work at the front desk of the Midwest Palms Motel.

I searched for the right words, immediately trying to figure out how to get out of it, even though I didn't have any reason to.

"I've never done either of those things," was what I settled on, perhaps the least cool combination of words my brain could put together.

She shucked the rest of the way out of her shirt, draping it over an arm, leaving her in a tank top and no bra.

"Like I said, you don't have to. Just thought it could be fun to hang out. I've been here for a month and I've barely talked to anyone except the landlords and they're . . . not fun."

I didn't have any excuses at the ready because nobody ever invited me to do anything.

"Okay," I said. "I gotta finish cleaning this room and run home—"

"Oh, that's fine," she said. "I didn't mean, like, right now. I'm gonna go home and take a fat nap anyway."

I'd been too eager and overbearing and became immediately flustered.

"Stupid me." I rolled my eyes, dissatisfied with myself. "You *said* later."

"You don't have to work tomorrow, do you?"

"I do but I don't come in til later."

"All right. You drive?"

I nodded.

"Bring beer?"

"Uh . . . sure."

"What's your number? I'll text you when I get up from my nap."

"I don't have one." Again, shame and embarrassment. "I mean, we have a landline."

"Okay. I can just call."

"Maybe . . . give me your number and I'll call you." I wasn't without a phone only because I was poor, I also couldn't imagine being tethered to my mom when I wasn't home. Work was the only place I went and Mom still managed to call the motel at least three times a week. Marnie would eventually know this, if she didn't already. She would become acquainted with Doris Milligan.

"One minute, please." She disappeared from the doorway and came back with her number written on a small, lined piece of paper torn from a Dollar General notebook, what passed for motel stationery here.

I didn't recognize the area code.

"It's a California number. Long story."

I blushed and tried to smile. I put the number in the pocket of my worn jeans.

"Okay. See ya later." Marnie flashed a quick, effortless smile before heading out to her car. A few men who were part of the crew renovating rooms at the motel openly leered at her. They were probably harmless but still made me uneasy. I already felt closer to Marnie than anyone else in years.

TWO

It was full dark by the time I got to Marnie's. I bought a six-pack of Miller Lite because it seemed popular and I didn't really know anything about beer. I felt like the clerk was judging me. He looked barely old enough to be selling beer. If I were an alcoholic or even just a habitual drinker, I'd have to buy it in another town. Hyte only had a couple thousand residents and I felt judged by most of them already. It was why the Midwest Palms was the ideal place for me. Being a housekeeper, I didn't have to interact with many of the guests and most of them were from out of town or just passing through. If I happened to recognize someone from town, they weren't going to mention anything because, if they were at the motel, they were doing something they didn't want anyone else to know about. It wasn't a daily occurrence but it happened enough. Maybe that was why some people liked living in these tiny towns. Your secrets were never really as secret as you thought they were and there was something liberating about that. Like going to confessional or something. And maybe I'd found my place in the town. A quiet woman pushing thirty with no friends and a zealous fear of drama. I didn't even write this stuff down in a journal. I supposed I could have paid for a laptop and found someplace online where motel workers dished on all the crazy things they saw but felt like it would be a waste of time. I had more important things to do, like tend to my mother and lie around in a depressed stupor.

Marnie's apartment was above a detached garage in the nicest section of Hyte. That didn't really mean anything. Mostly it was just a cul-de-sac where people had professional jobs, had their lawns mown or had the time and mental faculties to mow them, and could afford to replace a broken window with another window instead of plywood, cardboard, a Confederate flag, or an old Natty Light carton. There were dogs but they were the expensive kind or elderly pity rescues and usually on a leash or in the house. Most of the noise would come from people working in their yards, sounds of labor for the sake of status and beautification, and would not be noise made seemingly for the sole act of irritating those around you. These people knew how much they were paying to live here, no additional measures needed to be taken to assert their claim on their inconsequential acreage.

Marnie opened the door wearing the same basketball shorts and tank top she wore earlier. I held the beer out in front of me like it was an offering or something I couldn't wait to get rid of.

"You remembered!" she said. "This is definitely . . . beer."

I was immediately certain I'd made the wrong choice. "Is it okay?"

"It's *fine*. C'mon in."

I'd followed her instructions and taken a set of wooden stairs on the side of the garage to a door on the second floor or attic or whatever and now followed her through a fairly small apartment with the potential to be charming. I figured Marnie was not into "charming." At first glance, she seemed to be more into "comfort." The whole place smelled like cigarette and weed smoke and it looked like one of Marnie's life goals was to never put anything away.

"Sorry it's messy," Marnie said. "I'm a slob."

"I'm just glad you invited me." I hoped I didn't sound too desperate. "My place is worse." This was true. It was my mom who was the slob, not me. My room was usually spotless but that was just because I had a lot of nervous energy to burn off whenever I was home, which was whenever I wasn't at work.

"You ready?" Marnie said.

"Sure."

"We can order pizza or something later, if you're hungry."

"I ate when I got home from work. I'm okay."

"For *now*," Marnie said. "Take a seat." She motioned to a loveseat with a vibrantly colored green sheet thrown over it. I sat down and sank into it while Marnie put the beer in the fridge.

"Want one?" she called.

"Sure." I'd only had three beers in my life and those had all been consumed in the same night while I was in high school. Alone, while the rest of my class was at prom. They'd been in the refrigerator since before Dad moved away several years prior. I'd gotten sick and never had the desire to drink alcohol ever again.

The caps clinked into the trashcan and Marnie came back, handing me one of the bottles. I took a sip. It didn't taste good but it wasn't as bad as I remembered.

"I think I've heard of *Twin Peaks* but I've never seen it. What's it about?"

She took a much bigger sip of her beer and dug her fingers into her mess of dishwater blond hair she wore pulled back into a ponytail.

"I'm not great at explaining things. We'll just watch the pilot and if you like it maybe we can make a regular thing of watching the rest of it. It gets pretty wild."

"Sounds good to me."

She set her beer on a small, annihilated coffee table, took a DVD out of its case and loaded it into the machine.

She dropped down next to me on the loveseat, lit an American Spirit, and said, "Shit. You don't mind, do you?"

"Nah. My mom smokes. I'm used to it. Kind of like it, actually."

"Thanks, Lib. You're cool." She patted me on the knee. I twitched. "Shit," she said. "I'm sorry. You're jumpy."

I nervously exhaled and tried to smile. "Pretty much all the time, yeah."

"You wanna smoke some pot before we watch it? It'd take the edge off."

"I'm afraid it'd put me to sleep. I think the edge is permanent."

"All right. Here we go."

She navigated the screen to play the pilot.

There was something about the opening that felt immediately off. I knew *Twin Peaks* was a TV show. I thought it was from the eighties or early nineties. It was before my time. I thought most openings from back in the day had something to do with the show but this was just really sad-sounding music over depressing images of things like the sharpening of an industrial saw, a factory, a really big log, and the town sign boasting a population of 51,201 followed by a gorgeous waterfall. There was also a bird. It all seemed more fitting for a documentary about lumberjacks. I took another sip of beer, intrigued.

I didn't last long.

My body tensed up at the first shot of the plastic-wrapped body on the shore. The moisture left my mouth and I had to bear down so I wasn't noticeably shaking. I sucked down most of the rest of my beer to wet my mouth as much as anything. If it numbed me a little, that wasn't such a bad thing either. By the time it got to the part where the cop pulls back the plastic to reveal an attractive teenage girl, it felt like my stomach was dropping out of my body.

"How bout that weed?" I said.

Marnie belched. "I'm always ready for that."

She reached over and opened a drawer from the end table, producing a loaded, black ceramic pipe. She held it out to me.

"You better go first," I said.

"This is from back home where it's *legal*. Pretty strong shit."

She took a rip and handed the pipe to me while holding it in.

I took the same size hit.

I watched her until the pipe was cashed.

I turned back to the TV, unable to focus or concentrate. Perfect. Before I knew it, all tension had drained from my body. I leaned my head back on the loveseat and watched the colors flicker across the ceiling. I told myself I shouldn't close my eyes but did anyway and, the next thing I knew, birds were chirping and the small room was alight with the first glow of dawn.

Oddly, I felt very well rested. And panicked. Anxiety returned to squeeze my chest like an old friend.

"Shit," I said. "Shit. Shit. Shit."

I patted my pocket to make sure my keys were still there. The remaining beers, empty, were on the coffee table. I walked back to Marnie's bedroom. I felt weird entering and probably wouldn't have if the door hadn't been wide open.

I shook her. "I gotta go."

"Mmm." She seemed groggy but was doing better than me if I'd had five beers.

"Why didn't you wake me up?"

She smiled a little, covering her mouth with the back of her hand, and said, "You looked so *peaceful.*"

I couldn't really be mad at her. "Sorry, but I need to get home."

"You okay to drive?"

"I'm fine."

"Talk later?"

"Yeah. Okay. See ya."

THREE

Pulling into the driveway, the sinking feeling I'd had in my gut after realizing I'd overslept at Marnie's did not go unjustified. The car's lights flashed on the house. My mother had opened the front door and now stood pressed against the glass of the storm door. As I got out of the car and drew closer, the wildness in her eyes became more evident. I needed to choose my excuse carefully. Whatever I told her would be met with rage, but if I told her the truth, it would be thrown in my face for months or possibly years to come.

I opened the door, a little surprised she hadn't locked me out.

"I'm out of cigarettes." She was tensed up, arms held out from her body like she was ready to get in a bar fight.

"You need to move so I can get in."

"Smoked my last one toward the end of the news. Ain't had none since. Looked all over. Thought I might find a couple I'd forgotten about. Looked *all over.* Couldn't find a thing. Well, I guess you know why when you're stealing all the ones I leave behind. I guess one here and one there and you don't think I'll notice, huh?" She lowered her arms to her sides, her right hand beating out a tremor against her thigh.

"I'm not stealing your cigarettes, Mom. I'm not a kid. I can buy my own. I buy *yours.*"

"Do you have some for me?"

"No. I . . . I've been kind of busy and I'm tired. Please get out of the way."

"Price of admission is one pack of cigarettes."

I rolled my eyes. "Can't you just go to bed and I'll get you some before I go to work?"

She balled up her fists and shook her arms like an angry toddler. "I can't sleep unless I've had my last cigarette."

"The sun's already coming up."

"You want in this house, you better have cigarettes."

Too tired to fight, I threw my arms up and said, "Fine. Got any money for me?"

She reached into the pocket of her heavily stained and well-worn housecoat and pulled out a crumpled and slightly damp ten-dollar bill.

"Why don't you just give me money for a carton?"

"What if I want to quit?" She was completely serious when she said this. "I'll never quit if I have nine more packs laying around."

I never vocalized my thought that she wasn't going to quit. If I did, she would use that as an excuse not to quit, saying something like, "I could probably do it if anybody had any *faith* in me."

I took the money and said, "Be back in a bit."

"Hurry up. I need to smoke and get back to bed."

As I turned to walk to my car, I didn't expect a thank you or anything, nor would I expect one when I returned. I drove out to the all-night gas station located within sight of the motel. Sometimes, when I thought about my existence, the word "claustrophobic" came to mind. The clerk was unfamiliar to me because I'd never been there at this hour. I used my debit card to buy a carton of cigarettes I'd ration out to my mother, not knowing why I'd never thought to do this before. She never asked for change, so I'd turn a small profit, as well. I left the gas station feeling like a genius. Before getting back in the car, I glanced over at the motel. It seemed quiet, no more than ten cars in the parking lot. Maybe my late shift would be an easy one. When I got back home, Mom wasn't in front of the door anymore. She was sound asleep on the couch in front of a television filled with people who were way too chipper and alert for this hour. I put the pack of cigarettes on her lap.

FOUR

"Hey," Marnie said. Again, she'd come up behind me. Again, I was startled and dropped what I held, this time a roll of toilet paper that landed in the toilet with a splash.

We both stood there laughing at it.

"Want to go smoke with me before I clock in?"

I looked at the roll of toilet paper.

"Let it get soggy," Marnie said. "It'll be easier to get out."

I almost asked her why until realizing she wasn't serious.

"Who's in the office?" I asked.

"Rajat," she said. "He won't care."

I followed Marnie out of the room. Again, she wore the silvery basketball shorts and the stylish button-down shirt like she was dressed for a video conference.

The Midwest Palms Motel was your standard one-story, squared-U-shaped motel. What probably used to be called a motor court. Back when sleeping ten feet from your car was cool and not trashy. I was in the room directly opposite the office. Rajat was the owner's son, still a teenager, and didn't give a shit about anything. If Harry, his father, saw me taking a break, he would either ask me why I didn't clock out or go ahead and deduct ten minutes from my pay. He was kind of an asshole. I'd seen him rent rooms for as cheap as fifteen bucks a night just to fill up the motel but hadn't gotten a raise in the eight years I'd worked there. I'd never asked but was pretty sure I didn't even accumulate any sick leave or vacation days since I'd never been paid for the few days I'd had to call in.

Marnie sat down on one of the benches located between every other room. She took a cigarette from the box and offered it to me. I shook my head. She lit her cigarette and blew smoke out into the humid afternoon.

"It's gonna be hot," she said.

I squinted up into the low gray sky. "Supposed to storm later."

The motel and parking lot were surrounded by trees—several huge palms and some other trees more indigenous to the area—the greenness especially vibrant against the slate sky. No one seemed curious about the palms growing in the middle of Ohio and I'd never asked about them either. The sign for the motel was higher than most so it could be seen from the highway, even though it was a couple miles from it.

"I *love* storms." Marnie drew on her cigarette and studied the sign. "That sign is like . . . really tall." Nothing about the palms.

"Look . . ." I said. "About the other night . . ."

She patted me on the knee. "Don't worry about it. I shouldn't have let you get that high. I probably got too high too. Sorry you hated *Twin Peaks*. That was a dumb choice. It's too fuckin weird . . . and kind of disturbing."

I tried to smile but it felt pained. "It's not that . . ." I paused. "Actually, maybe it is kind of that. Not that I hated it. I don't think I saw enough of it to hate it. I just couldn't watch it." I knew my smile had faded completely, my mind back on that fall night shortly after we'd moved to the house where Mom and I still lived. All I had to do was close my eyes and I was right there.

I glanced toward the office to see Rajat exiting and walking toward us.

I patted Marnie on the bare knee, her skin slightly sticky from the humidity but still electric against my palm.

"Maybe I'll swing by the office and talk to you later," I said.

"I'll probably be bored out of my fucking skull."

"Good afternoon, ladies." Rajat always dressed well and wore expensive cologne that would have smelled good if he didn't wear so much of it. Crossing the parking lot had caused him to break a sweat.

"Busy today?" Marnie took another casual drag from her cigarette.

Rajat laughed and made a sweeping gesture around the mostly empty parking lot. The only vehicles in it were mine, Marnie's, and the heavy-duty trucks and semi-trailer belonging to the Seabliss Renovation Company. "Does it look like it?"

"I was kind of joking," Marnie said.

"I'm going to get back to cleaning. Only two rooms left."

As I disappeared into the room, I heard Rajat say, "Be careful with that one," and I could practically see him cranking his index finger around his temple in the universal gesture for crazy. I knew Marnie wouldn't take his advice. She was probably crazier than me. She was, I guessed, nearly thirty, looked like a model, and had moved to this shithole town to live above a garage. There was definitely a story there. As with most things in my life, I imagined the story would come to an abrupt end before I wanted it to and I'd be left with a sense of longing and confusion before returning to the unbroken sameness I was more accustomed to.

FIVE

"You're soaked." Marnie sat on the couch in front of the big screen TV in the tiny lobby, her bare feet up on the coffee table, a lot of pale leg exposed.

"No shit." Turns out we hadn't gotten thunderstorms, just a bunch of rain.

I clocked out on the computer behind the front desk and grabbed a towel from a linen cabinet we kept stocked for the one guest per night who needed more towels than most humans on the planet. Or, more likely, the towels they had in their room were horribly stained or covered in pubic hair. I tied my wet hair up in it so I didn't have to feel it on the back of my neck and sat next to Marnie. She was watching *Leap Frog*, a fairly simple-minded reality show featuring out-of-work celebrities playing the most mean-spirited match of leap frog the show's producers could think of.

"Is that Charlie Sheen?" I said.

"Yeah." Marnie smiled.

"Who's the other guy?"

"He's from some band I've never heard of called the Spin Doctors. I don't remember what they said his name was. I guess he's known for this song." She turned the TV up and the lobby filled with an extremely catchy but also kind of lame-sounding pop song. "They have to leap frog around the room, drink a liter of water, and then do it again. The first one who pisses himself loses."

"Sounds degrading."

"I'm sure they love it."

The rain continued to hammer down outside as we sat mesmerized in front of the glowing TV.

Marnie placed a hand on my knee and shook my leg back and forth.

"You kind of acted like you wanted to tell me something earlier."

"*Yeah.*" I attempted a half-hearted smile. "It's . . . a lot. I feel like I should just put it out there though, so you don't feel like you're getting to know a remotely normal person."

"Who likes normal people?"

"Not here. I don't want to get interrupted. I'll freeze up and talk myself out of saying anything."

"Hold up then." She got off the couch and went behind the counter. When she returned to the couch, she said, "There. I think we'll be okay."

"What did you do?"

"Turned the 'No Vacancy' sign on."

"Startlingly simple." For as long as I'd worked there, it had never occurred to me the Vacancy/No Vacancy sign was an independently controlled thing. A naïve part of my brain thought it only came on when the motel was actually full.

I got a cup of coffee and went outside to sit with Marnie under the awning while she smoked a cigarette.

I told her my story.

SIX

When I was ten, my world fell apart. One Friday night in September, after a football game, my older sister, Lauren, went missing. I barely knew what that meant, could barely process the tension that strangled our house like a zip tie suddenly tightened. Looking back on it, I can only think of the liquidity of that word—"missing." It sounds bad, right? Nobody wants anything to be missing. But think of it this way—if something's missing, you don't know for sure someone has stolen it, you don't know for sure it's broken, you don't know for sure it's dead. When I think of that word now, that's how I define it—"missing" means "not dead." And, of course, the opposite of "missing" is "found," which most people probably see as a positive term. But Lauren was dead when they found her. "Found," to me, means "dead." Lauren was in a bare cornfield, her body wrapped in plastic. Lauren Milligan seen as Laura Palmer nearly sixteen years after her death. I think Marnie began to understand why I freaked out.

After they found her body, my parents' marriage didn't stand a chance. My dad lost his job. Mom refused to leave the house. Eventually my dad split to live with his family in West Virginia. I haven't seen him since. As much as I don't want to, I get it. It's too painful. I feel the same way. Sometimes the absence of two people is, oddly, less painful than the absence of one. Like, if I still had him in my life, that would mean the family unit was almost complete . . . except for Lauren. Dad's absence mitigated the grief.

My parents were still in the process of fixing the house up when Dad left. It still looked like we'd never completely moved in. Mom had not stepped foot out of it since Lauren's death. She relied on me to bring her things and panicked if I wasn't there when she knew I should be. Since I had no life, that was whenever I wasn't at work or running errands for her.

We all dealt with the murder of Lauren in the worst ways possible. We just didn't talk about it. I knew there was a massive investigation, and I remember seeing the newspaper articles starting on page one and, gradually, over the weeks, how those articles started to slide further back in the paper like a metaphor for minimizing trauma. People stopped visiting. People stopped asking my mom about it. I served out my middle and high school years as the weird girl with the dead sister. Now I was a twenty-six-year-old woman with no friends who lived with her agoraphobic mother and had never had sex, never kissed anyone, never even held hands with anyone, never been on a date, and the first time I ever got high was with Marnie a couple days ago.

I didn't cry when I told her this. Probably exhibited an eerie lack of emotion. I was still numb. I understood this. When you live your life mostly separate from humanity, you feel like an alien when you try to understand the emotional landscapes of other humans. There's a disconnect.

When I finished talking, Marnie plucked one of my hands out of my lap and put it in her larger hand.

Then I let myself cry.

SEVEN

Back outside, Marnie smoked another cigarette. The rain had stopped, the air now hot and muggy, a palpable thing.

"I remember that," Marnie said. "I was kind of obsessed with it. Maybe that's why I became obsessed with *Twin Peaks*. I went to high school with Lauren. Don't know why I didn't put two and two together. I'm sorry. I'm stupid."

"I thought you were from California."

"I was there a while. I'm from right here so . . . I should have known."

"How could you have?"

"I didn't think there was any way you and your mom would still be here."

"Well, there was no way I was getting my mom out of here. It's like she's just waiting for somebody to come knocking on the door to explain everything that happened to her. Hell, some days she talks about Lauren like she's still alive. Maybe she's still waiting for her to come back."

Marnie took the last drag of her cigarette and stuck it in the sand of the ashtray.

"Let's get back inside," she said. "It's gross out here."

I followed her into the blessed air conditioning of the lobby.

Marnie had said a couple things that didn't set in until we were inside.

Marnie had gone to school with Lauren. She said she'd been obsessed with the case. Did she know anything? I wasn't sure it was a box I wanted to open. If the cops hadn't found anything out in sixteen years, I didn't think I stood much of a chance now. I knew I should just let it lie but found myself lingering in the lobby, making small talk with Marnie and watching stupid shit on the TV. Being around her made me feel lighter. It made the thought of going home absolutely oppressive. I thought about what I'd just put on her and figured she probably felt completely opposite about my presence. I wondered if she didn't see me as something like a sad, dark quilt, ready to suck the life from her carefree existence. Of course, I knew it couldn't be that carefree and now wondered if I wanted to know the truth of why she came back.

I went to the breakfast station and got another cup of coffee.

"So . . . you said you were obsessed with my sister's case?" I asked.

"We all were," Marnie said.

"Who's 'we'?"

"Like just about every girl in the high school. I was a few years younger than your sister. She was a junior when it happened, right?"

I nodded.

"And I was a freshman."

"I thought you were younger than me."

She winked and said, "I get plenty of sleep, mostly avoid food and men, have never been pregnant, and never worked hard. Not a day in my life."

"What were people saying about it then?"

"I still have the scrapbooks."

"The scrapbooks?"

"And my journal."

"You kept a journal?"

"I told you I was kind of obsessed with it. That happened toward the beginning of the schoolyear. I paid close attention to it until the spring when one of my friends encouraged me to go out for the track team. I think she'd decided my obsession was unhealthy. Not long after that I got my first boyfriend and that was all I could think about all summer. You can come over and take a look at them if you want."

"Maybe." I sipped my coffee. The warmth was nice. The lobby felt too cold now. "Did you or your friends have any idea what happened to her?"

Marnie nodded. "*Everyone* seemed to have a theory. Most of them didn't make any real sense. There were the obvious assumptions that it was a boyfriend but, as far as I knew, your sister never had a boyfriend. She seemed virginal. Maybe another reason I became obsessed with *Twin Peaks* when I first found out about it. Cause Laura's seen as this good girl, right? But she's totally fucked up. And I do have to say that watching *Twin Peaks* for the first time got me thinking about your sister again. It was the only angle I wasn't really able to explore."

"What angle's that?"

"The family angle."

"The family angle?"

"Okay, spoiler alert . . ." Marnie again plucked my hand out of my lap and held it between both of hers and I didn't know if it felt so good because I was starting to see her as a surrogate big sister or if it felt good for some other reason. "Laura Palmer was so fucked up because her father had been raping her. There's a whole lot more to it, but that's the gist of it. And, ultimately, it was her father who murdered her while in some kind of schizo-psychotic fugue. Basically, he's possessed by an entity called Bob. It's kind of unclear if Bob is, like, from another dimension or an aspect of Laura's father who, otherwise, was a very respected member of the community. Like I said though, I wasn't able to pursue that. Your parents wouldn't talk to me and I figured the police would have worked that angle pretty hard. I mean, they must have asked you if your parents were abusive or if you had any relatives that touch you in your swimsuit area."

I stared blankly at the TV and said, "If they did, I have no recollection of it."

"You have no recollection of the cops or social workers or whatever asking or you have no recollection of being touched?"

"Ew," I said. "No. I would have remembered that. My dad was just angry white trash. I don't remember him being pervy."

"But he did split pretty soon afterward. Didn't look good."

"He left because my mother was intolerable."

"And you're probably right. Like I said, I was pretty sure that was an angle the cops had exhausted thoroughly."

"Any other theories?"

"A jealous girl was one we'd knocked around but, you know, if some kind of rivalry had gotten to that point, somebody would have been talking about it. Also, Lauren wasn't a competitive person. Sure, she probably had the best grades in the school but teenagers don't care about that shit. She didn't play sports or date anybody so I can't see anyone being jealous enough of her to want to kill her."

"Makes sense," I said. "I can't remember her ever talking shit about anyone."

"So I was left with chalking it up to random violence."

"What do you mean?"

"Bad luck. Being in the wrong place at the wrong time. A pretty girl who just happened to catch the eye of a passing psychopath."

I found Marnie's words as comforting as the black coffee. This was the same basic theory I'd had. If the murder were to remain unsolved, it seemed like the best theory to live with. No one wants to think there might be a monster in their town or, even worse, their family. No one wants to think anything like that can happen again. No one wants to think it could have been one of them. Better for it to be the unfamiliar, some random stranger passing through. Sure, he would probably repeat the crime, but it would be somewhere very far away, happening to someone as faceless and anonymous as the stranger himself. Yes, "*himself*," because no one imagined a woman capable of snuffing the life out of someone as precious as Lauren Milligan.

"I think I'd like that," I said, not knowing if it was because I really wanted to live through that time period again or if I just wanted to spend another evening with Marnie.

"Sorry. Like what?"

"To look at your scrapbooks and stuff."

"Any night's good with me. Not a lot going on."

"Tonight cool?"

"I don't get off til midnight and, honestly, I'm probably just going to go home, get high out of my mind, and pass out in front of the TV."

"You're off tomorrow, right?" I cringed while saying it, making it obvious I'd memorized her schedule.

When she said, "But you're not," it made me feel a little better.

"Yeah, but I'll be off by five. I can just come by after."

"Works for me."

Something distracted Marnie. She stared toward the entrance. I turned to follow her gaze.

"What the hell?" Marnie said.

A stooped old man wearing an ancient black raincoat dug through the ashtray.

"Oh," I said. "That's just Drifter Ken. He wanders out of the woods or down the highway or something. He's harmless. If he irritates you, just tell him Harry told him he couldn't be on the property. Nobody ever runs him off. He's just looking for butts."

He didn't glance up from the ashtray, totally in his own world. He pocketed a few butts and shambled through the parking lot in the direction of the main road.

EIGHT

I came home and threw a pack of cigarettes on the table. Mom had given me ten bucks that morning and I'd taken the pack from the carton living in my glove compartment, glad cigarette manufacturers weren't compelled to put the "Not Available for Individual Sale" disclaimers on their packs.

It was like Mom knew I had something else going on. I could feel her need ramping up.

"Lib!" she called out from the living room as I was on my way to my bedroom to hide. I halted, contemplating continuing on and pretending I didn't hear her.

I stopped and went into the living room to see what she wanted. Maybe talking to Marnie about Lauren's case had made me more sympathetic toward her. Maybe the tingle of excitement I felt about going to Marnie's tomorrow made me feel more resilient. It had been so long since I'd been excited for anything. Graduating high school and knowing I didn't have to go back was probably the last time. I didn't even get excited the few times a guest had hit on me at the motel. It just felt gross and usually a little frightening since it was typically just them and me in a room with nobody else around.

Mom sat in the darkened living room, the TV flickering with a

Lifetime movie called *Nineteen Abortions*.

"Want me to bring your cigarettes to you?"

She brought up a throatful of phlegm with a brief, powerful hack and said, "Would you, please?"

I went back into the kitchen, grabbed the pack from the table, and tossed them to her. They landed on the hammock created by her gown stretched between her two bony thighs.

"Come and sit down." She raked a pile of undetermined papers from the couch and onto the floor.

The worst thing about living with her and having no life was that I rarely had a legitimate argument to get out of these things. My default excuse was that I had to go take a shower but she knew as well as I that I could do that at any time. It wasn't like I rolled around in feces all day. Well, not the good days, anyway.

I huffed, because that's pretty much what I'd done since I was twelve, before sitting next to her.

"I thought only sociopaths watched things like this," I said.

Mom was perhaps the most humorless person I knew. I wasn't gifted in that department either but I was at least capable of knowing when someone made a joke or said something funny and demonstrating at least some form of response. The current scene on the TV was of a wholesomely attractive twenty-something woman standing on a curb and crying, a building clearly labeled "Abortion Clinic" behind her. It was so sentimental, pandering, and factually incorrect, I didn't see how anyone could find it anything *but* funny . . . or insulting.

"She's waiting for her boyfriend to pick her up," Mom said. "She's sad because she got the abortion because he wanted her to and now it looks like he's not even going to pick her up. This is the third time she's been tricked into getting an abortion."

I stifled my laughter. Mom lit a cigarette.

"And this, I'm guessing, happens sixteen more times?"

"I don't know. I haven't seen this one. My guess is that the nineteenth abortion doesn't happen. That'll probably be the man of her dreams."

"How have the abortions been?"

"What do you mean?"

"I mean, are they like really detailed?"

"Pretty graphic, I guess. Real emotional."

"I might stick around until I get to see one of those but then I need to take a shower and get to bed. Gotta get to work a little early tomorrow."

"Think you could stop by the store? We're low on just about everything." And now we'd come to the real reason she'd called me in here. "There's a list on the fridge."

"Can it wait til Thursday? It's like one more day."

"I'm out of cookies and there's not much milk left."

"Yeah, but there's plenty of stuff to eat and drink, right? You're not going to starve."

A tremor ran through her right hand and she quickly transferred the cigarette to her left. I could almost predict what she said next, word-for-word: "I just got my habits, you know? I get all twitchy when they're disrupted."

"Fine. But it might be a little later."

"How much later?"

"I don't know. Later than usual."

"Why?"

"I have other things to do."

"Oh . . . with who?" And I could see that derisive gleam in her eye without even looking at her. "That new girl at the motel? Sounds friendly. Little familiar. She from in town?"

"No. California. And no, I don't have plans with her. You know I don't have any friends."

"That's cause you're all mine." She leaned over toward me, the closest thing I ever got to a hug, and I focused on her claw-like hand squeezing her bony knee tightly to keep it from trembling.

NINE

Things at the motel ended up being really slow so I decided to get Mom's shit after work because I thought three in the afternoon would be an odd time to go to Marnie's. She didn't have to work today so it was highly likely she wouldn't have even been awake. Mom performed the usual act to keep me from going back out, saying she wasn't feeling well and what would she do if she needed to go to the hospital? I'd never taken her to the hospital before, as that would have required leaving the house. I told her she would have to call 911 for an ambulance and explain to them she was agoraphobic and Mom stared at me like she didn't know what any of those things meant. I knew none of this would happen. She was as hesitant to let people into the house as she was to leave it. Plus she hated to call people unless it was me at the motel.

I had to lie to her, something I didn't particularly mind doing. My lies had to be elaborate enough to dissuade her from calling but couldn't involve anything that might resemble fun. I told her I had to clean up a couple of the renovated rooms because Harry wanted them available for the morning.

"I won't be able to come to the phone."

Mom rolled her eyes and looked as trapped as she always did. "Those people need to treat you better. Or you need a better *job*."

"To get a better job, I'd have to move out of Hyte and leave you alone." I both did and did not feel bad making Mom sound like a burden.

"Just be careful. I worry about you there with all them construction workers."

"I hardly see them."

This was mostly true. But I was sure, if I were actually at the motel after dark, I would definitely hear them. Cleaning their rooms revealed a lot about their previous night's excess. There weren't any bars near the motel, so the workers seemingly turned each of their rooms into a personal bar/strip club. While I was cleaning rooms, they were mostly off in other rooms doing their renovations. They were clearly starved for female companionship but my demeanor was so off-putting only a couple of them had ever tried talking to me.

Mom's expression turned dismissive and she waved me away with one hand while the other clutched her thigh.

I bought a bottle of wine at the grocery store to take to Marnie's. It felt like an adult thing to do. Even though I was pretty sure I might need it after digging through the memories of my sister's death, I didn't think weed was for me and thought it would seem less square to say I didn't want to mix the two. Of course, I'd never drank wine before and wasn't prepared for how rancid it was. At least it would keep me from overdoing it. Marnie had rinsed out a red Solo cup and filled it halfway and I felt like that might last me the entire evening.

"I'm sorry," I said. "This is awful."

Marnie shrugged. "It's not too bad. Not a big wine person myself but alcohol's alcohol."

Eventually, I would remember to ask her why she'd come back to Hyte.

"You ready to look?" she said.

I took a deep breath. I'd been thinking about it in a soft, peripheral way ever since she'd mentioned it but I still wasn't sure if I was ready.

"Honestly," I said, "I don't think I'll ever be ready."

"You don't have to."

"I feel like I should."

"I know it hurts."

She reached out and put a hand on my shoulder and it was like the smallest act of her trying to comfort me shook something loose and, before I knew it, I took a step into her now open arms and let myself be pulled into her, feeling her breasts press into my chest, wrapping my arms around her slender torso and feeling the heat of her back on my palms. I let the tears run down my cheeks and sink into her t-shirt. She hugged me until I broke the embrace.

"Why are you being so nice to me?" I said.

"Because you're a friend," she said. "I don't know. I guess friends are nice to each other. Trust me, if you'd ever gotten out of this shitty town, you'd have all kinds of friends. You're not a hideous freak."

"That's what I act like, isn't it?"

"Maybe a little. You act like someone who thinks they're useless, as a person. You keep your head down and do what you have to do to get by. People notice this. You're closed off. It's like you feel like you don't deserve friends or to have fun or anything and . . . well, people are lazy, so nobody's going to work that hard to crack your shell."

"Except you."

She pulled a cigarette from her pack and let it dangle from a corner of her mouth. "I don't think I've worked that hard. Maybe we just met at the right time."

Why did you come back? The question was right there on the tip of my tongue.

She lit her cigarette and said, "Come on, everything's in my room."

It wasn't until I'd followed her into her bedroom to retrieve one large scrapbook and a couple of shoeboxes and then back out into the living room that I noticed she'd cleaned considerably since the last time I was here. Coming from my mother's hoarder den, it was oddly unnerving.

"And, you know," she said, "if it gets to be too much, we can stop and find something stupid to watch. Okay?"

"Kay."

She set everything on the coffee table, remarkably graced with nothing except an ashtray. I suddenly found myself a lot more nervous than I thought I'd be.

"Doing okay?" she asked.

"Yeah . . . Just freaking out a little."

I took a sip of the wine, hoping it would have an instantaneous effect. It didn't.

"Maybe start with this." She pushed the thick scrapbook over to me. It had a black faux-leather cover and looked more like something a burgeoning Wiccan would use to collect recipes and spells.

I opened it to see the headline that had been seared into my brain.

"BODY WRAPPED IN PLASTIC"

I continued flipping through the scrapbook while Marnie pulled random articles and scraps of paper from the shoeboxes. While I read through the headlines and scanned the articles, I felt less a feeling of sadness—what I thought I'd feel—and more a feeling of anger. All the articles were so impersonal I had to remind myself they were about my sister. Based on the articles, if I hadn't known her, I would have thought her name was Seventeen-year-old Female. The anger continued to build as I neared the end of the scrapbook, my glass of wine only half-depleted. I had thought my parents had sheltered me from this kind of thing at the time but just the headlines were enough to remind me I'd read most of the articles before. I'd just filed it all away. I hadn't really forgotten any of it.

I reached the end of the scrapbook and handed it back to Marnie. She scooted a stack of smaller, more random clippings over to me.

"These are some articles from other papers and magazines across the country," she said.

I took another sip of wine and began leafing through them. There was nothing new. If anything, they were even more anonymous and frustrating. At seventeen, Lauren had probably been too old for her case to reach fever pitch at a national level.

By the time I'd flipped through them as quickly as a boy flipping through his baseball card collection, more than two hours had passed and Marnie and I had hardly spoken.

"So?" she said after I'd spent what felt like a half hour staring into my wine.

"What do you want me to say?"

"Just say *something*." She tried to force a smile. "You got so quiet."

"I'm glad you did this."

"Why?"

"It makes me feel like someone cares. Like someone besides me and my mom and my dad ever cared." I tried to find the words to make this make sense. "All the articles sound so cold. Almost accusatory. Like it's her fault. We were never what you would call a respected family and I'm not even sure how much the cops cared. After she was found . . . I felt so separated from everyone at school so . . . it's really nice that it could bring us together like this." And now maybe the wine was getting to me because I *did* start tearing up. But not about my sister. It was because Marnie was being so nice to me. I decided to let her know that, again, before breaking down into a small blubbering fit. "Just . . . thank you for being so nice to me."

Further back in my brain but still there, that thought: *Why did you come back?*

Marnie once again took me into her arms and let me cry it out. When I was finished, I pulled away from her and said, "I should go."

"Stick around," she said. "I'll order a pizza. There's still like nearly a half-full bottle of wine in there."

I said, "Yeah, maybe I'm just hungry. Maybe that's why the wine is hitting me so hard," just to be saying something.

Marnie said, "Pizza always helps," instead of telling me I was buzzed from a half glass of wine because I was a lightweight and practically still a fucking child.

Marnie dug her phone out of the couch cushions and called in the pizza. Oddly, I thought about my mother and felt like she would almost be able to live on her own if she embraced technology.

"Sorry if that brought back some bad memories," Marnie said.

I shrugged and said, "They were all there anyway."

"Nothing new?"

"Not to me."

"Now I feel like I did a bad job. Look, I really felt like an amateur sleuth at the time, okay?"

I took another sip of wine and looked into Marnie's deep blue eyes. "Did you . . .?" I didn't know if I wanted to ask.

"Did I what?"

"Did you find it . . . exciting? I mean, I wouldn't be mad at you if you did. I'd get it. She wasn't your sister."

"Exciting? Probably. I don't know if that's the exact right word . . ." She paused and lit a cigarette, her hand shaking slightly. "You're not the only one who's fucked up, okay? I mean, I think I'm a lot better now but . . . at the time . . . let me put some thoughts together and get back to you."

"You can tell me anything."

"I know," she said. "Maybe just not right now." She placed her free hand over mine and said, "I'm not trying to keep anything from you."

"When you're ready," I said. "You mentioned a journal . . ."

She rolled her eyes. "I looked through it last night. Too embarrassing. There wasn't as much in there about your sister as I'd thought."

"That's okay."

"I mean, I was fourteen, okay? And definitely *not* a writer."

"It's okay. I understand."

"You know how you think *everything* is important when you're that age."

I laughed a little. "It's really okay. It's too personal."

"It's not even that. It's just . . . *bad*. I apparently spent a lot of time thinking about my period and analyzing Beatles lyrics."

"Oof."

"I know, right?"

The pizza came shortly thereafter and we crushed the entire thing, greatly increased our wine intake, and watched part of a marathon TV show about a guy who works at McDonald's and keeps losing his teeth while also working on the great American novel. The spin is that he has an MIT degree in engineering and could easily make more money and be a benefit to society by doing something with that. I was pretty sure it was about sacrifice. Or maybe narcissism or ego or the lack thereof. I didn't really know. If it hadn't been for the studio audience, I wouldn't have known when to laugh.

The wine bottle had been emptied and I only had a couple of sips left in my glass.

Marnie rolled a joint and sparked it up.

"What time is it?" I asked. There were no clocks anywhere and I didn't wear a watch.

Marnie checked the display of her phone and said, "9:53."

"I should probably be getting home." I thought if I left right now, I might be able to get home and into bed before passing out.

"You sure you're okay to drive? You know it's slim pickins for the cops in this town."

"I should be okay." I stood up and almost fell down.

Marnie laughed through a mouthful of smoke. "You are *not* okay. Go lay down in my bed for a couple hours. You'll feel better."

That sounded like a good idea.

TEN

Thunder woke me up, the lightning like a strobe light in the darkened room. I was groggy, my eyes half-closed. I was in Marnie's bed. So was Marnie, lying close to me, one of her hands on the back of my neck, her other hand down the front of my jeans, over the underwear, her lips pressed against my ear.

"What . . . what are you doing?" I struggled to speak. Her hand moved slowly against me, pressing the magic spot I hardly ever touched myself.

"Is this okay?" she whispered into my ear, her hot breath sending shivers down my spine.

"It's not . . . not okay but . . ."

Her hand stopped its massaging.

"I should go." I struggled to sit up.

"Please stay." She brought her hand up to my face. It smelled like me.

"I feel gross." I couldn't think of anything else to say.

"You're perfect," she said.

I snorted out a laugh and said, "Now I *know* you're crazy."

Then she moved her hand to squeeze both of my cheeks like I was a kid.

"You're not going anywhere," she said, "until you kiss me."

I closed my eyes and said, "I'd like that."

And her hands were on either side of my head and I'd never kissed anyone before, not like that, and her mouth was on mine, her tongue parting my lips and entering my mouth. She tasted like pizza, wine, weed, and cigarettes and I couldn't get enough of it. I knew it couldn't go any further and had to ask myself why. What would be the harm in it?

Marnie broke the kiss. "I could make you feel really good if you stay."

"I can't."

"It's not a scary thing."

"Feels pretty scary."

"I'm not going to pressure you."

"Will you . . . kiss me again?"

She got up on her elbow and swung a bare leg over me. Her basketball shorts were now off. She wore a pair of simple black underwear. She straddled my hips and leaned down and we kissed again and her hands slid up my shirt to play with my tits over my bra as she grinded her crotch against me. There was so little fabric separating us and everywhere she touched me was like a fire and I knew if I didn't make her stop, we would end up going through with it. Again, there was that part of me that asked why not and I was pretty sure I knew. Either way, I was going to have to get back home and if I were going to make her the first person I'd ever slept with, I wanted to wake up next to her. A stupid, romantic notion, I knew. I pulled away from her and she collapsed back onto my thighs, her shoulders slumping.

"Now you look sad," I said.

"I'm fucking *horny*, bitch," she joked. Her hand had left my face and now made slow circles around the crotch of her underwear.

"I'm sorry," I said. "I'm a weirdo."

"You don't know what you want. I don't want to pressure you."

I looked at her, admiring how not self-conscious she was. I imagined what would happen after I left—the underwear sliding down, probably not even all the way off, her spreading those long, skinny legs and opening the folds between them as she did what I could only bring myself to do in the shower, even though I knew it was nothing to be ashamed of or embarrassed about.

It occurred to me that I could touch her. As commanding as she was, she would probably let me do anything I wanted to her. But if I started that, I knew I wouldn't be leaving.

I reached out and ran my knuckles down the front of her tank top, stopping when I hit the band of pale flesh above her underwear.

"It's a good thing you didn't pressure," I said, "because I wouldn't have said no."

She hopped off and flopped onto her back, reached over to her nightstand and plucked a cigarette from her pack. She lit up, holding the cigarette in her right hand as her left continued to circle the surface of her underwear.

"You're driving me insane," she said.

"You're driving me insaner." I stood up, tugged my shirt down and wiggled around until I felt comfortable in my jeans again, conscious of her eyes on my body. That was why I couldn't go through with it. I still couldn't wrap my head around the idea of someone being physically attracted to me. It seemed ridiculous, like it had to be as inspired by cruelty as lust.

"You work tomorrow?" I already knew the answer.

"You know it. Bright and early."

She had a faraway look in her eye and I felt like I should probably leave her alone to do what she so clearly needed to.

"You can watch if you want," she said.

"I really have to get back."

Why did you *come back?*

"Then go," she said, the disappointment and frustration in her voice completely unmasked.

"I'm sorry," I said again.

"Please stop saying that. If you were truly sorry, my head would be between those legs right now."

I lowered my head and walked to the front door. There was no easing out of this situation.

I thought about her the entire way home. I threw myself around in my bed, unable to sleep. I masturbated, in bed, for the first time since I was a teenager but couldn't bring myself to orgasm. I never could, which was one of the reasons I hardly ever did it and probably one of the reasons I hadn't done anything with Marnie. I'd already told her I was a virgin but I was also pretty sure I was broken in some irreparable way.

I was still thinking about her when I woke up way too late the next morning.

ELEVEN

It was nearly noon by the time I got to the motel. Marnie was already there and there was no avoiding her. My face glowed a bright red the second I saw her sitting on the couch in the lobby.

"Who was here this morning when you came in?" I said, thinking my tardiness was a good excuse to avoid talking about the elephant in the room.

"Harry," Marnie yawned out. "He actually called me in at like six. I'm *so* tired."

"Cool. So he doesn't know I'm like four hours late. Shit. I'm going to be here until eight. Did we have a lot of check-outs?"

"Nearly every fucking room."

"Fuck. Seriously?"

"First Friday. The Columbus swingers, I guess?"

"The worst."

"Raj's supposed to relieve me around two. I'm gonna have to nap for a bit, but I could probably help you after that."

I was so used to the front desk workers thinking they were somehow better than the housekeeping staff that, even though it was Marnie, her offer was still shocking. It was beneath even anyone in Harry's family. His wife and daughter did it when I wasn't there but never once had he had them help me.

"That would help so much," I said. "I'll make it up to you."

"How?"

I was behind the desk, clocking in on the computer. She stood up from the couch and walked toward me. Given last night, I realized how what I'd said could be taken.

"I'll let you decide."

She leaned on the counter, drumming her fingertips against it. "I'll have to think of something good."

I grabbed the keys to the supply closet where the housekeeping cart was and started for the door.

"I'm sorry," she said out of nowhere.

I stopped and turned. "You don't have anything to be sorry about."

"I felt pushy after you left. It's okay if you're not into me or . . . girls or . . . whatever."

I'd thought about this quite a bit last night as I tossed and turned. I tried not to obsess on Marnie too much because I was pretty sure she had just been wasted and horny and would never mention it again and then I'd feel more like a loser for thinking about her so much.

I swallowed the lump in my throat. "I don't know what I'm into, really, but I'm very into you."

Then I was pretty sure I saw Marnie blush.

TWELVE

It's amazing how fast life can change. A family getting taken out by a drunk driver or fleeing a burning house. Someone finally getting that call about the test results. The morning we wake up to frequently looks far different than the night we leave behind.

And we never see it coming.

THIRTEEN

Carrying all the dirty linens out to the cart, I looked toward the office hoping to catch a glimpse of Marnie smoking a cigarette. She was out front talking to one of the guys from Seabliss Renovation. I couldn't hear what they were saying but Marnie looked perturbed and the guy looked almost angry. Eventually, he dug into his back pocket, pulled out his wallet, and handed Marnie some cash. I had no idea what was going on but felt like I witnessed some illicit transaction. After handing her the money, the guy turned and stomped off to one of the trucks. I put my head down and began pushing my cart to the next room so Marnie wouldn't think I was spying.

The room in between was one of the ones being renovated. The floor was covered in clear plastic and I heard a hammer and saw going. I glanced into the room to see two younger guys in tank tops and shorts. They both stopped what they were doing and glanced my way. When I'd crossed the door enough to be out of sight, one of them said, "Ain't never seen such a stuck-up maid."

To which the other responded, "Wouldn't mind her stickin that ass up in my face."

"I'd slap them titties around."

It sent a chill down my spine. I left my cart outside the next room but locked the door while I worked in there. I never understood why guys did that. They knew they were talking loud enough for me to hear them. Did they think it should be taken as some sort of compliment? Did they think I was going to dash back to their room, lift up my shirt, and say "Did someone say tits?" before some construction-themed gangbang broke out?

It flustered me so much I didn't think about Marnie and the other worker until I'd calmed down somewhat. I didn't want to think I was already jealous but something about it bothered me. It wasn't just the exchange. It was that he'd handed her money. I wanted to think Marnie wouldn't stoop to doing anything sexual for money but . . . well, I couldn't rule it out either. It depended on what she had less interest in—men or working—and I really didn't know her well enough to commit in either direction. I made a mental note to ask her about the dude in a way that wouldn't make it sound like I'd been watching her like a voyeuristic creep. For the time being, I calmed myself by thinking she had probably just sold him some drugs and wanted her money.

Turning to the room at hand, my first thought was that it had been destroyed by sex and I wondered how cautionary that was. White Claw cans were scattered all over. The smell of sex still lingered. There was an oppressively moist quality to it. The bodily fluids covering the sheet—the only thing on the bed—still looked wet and I couldn't help but think about Marnie and that man again. I never wore earbuds or listened to music while I cleaned rooms and wished I had some form of distraction at the moment. Instead, I just concentrated on trying to finish as fast as I could. There was still so much to do.

FOURTEEN

I had three rooms left. The sun was starting to sink and the air was intensely still and humid. I heard a shuffling sound behind me and turned to see Marnie approaching me in her basketball shorts and tank top, dragging her leg behind her.

"Are you okay?" I immediately had visions of the man from earlier returning to rough her up and get his money back.

She immediately straightened up and smiled. "That was my warning signal."

"Warning signal?"

"Yeah. I always feel like I'm sneaking up on you."

"So you thought it would be better to make me think you'd been horribly injured?"

"Hey, at least you didn't jump out of your skin this time."

"True, but that's probably because I'm exhausted."

"Sorry I'm late."

"No big deal. I've only got a few more to do."

"Raj let me take a nap in one of the rooms you'd already cleaned. I forgot to set an alarm. Napped for like three hours."

"Well, you missed the vomit party in the last room."

"Vomit party?"

"A very unfortunate vomit party. Thought about asking Raj if we could just have it permanently quarantined."

"That bad, huh?"

"Worse."

"Okay, boss, what do you want me to do?"

"Just help me out and we should be able to knock these out in an hour or so."

"Right!" Marnie snapped to attention and saluted me.

Only a few minutes into the next room, Marnie proved to be as bad at cleaning as I would have predicted. She worked quickly, at least, wanting to get out of here as badly as I did. I was firmly entrenched in my routine. It made it hard to maintain chit-chat with her and gave me a heavy feeling in my heart and a sensitivity bordering on discomfort between my legs. So the last three rooms were finished quickly, never mind if they were actually clean. The type of person who stayed here didn't have the highest of standards anyway. As long as there weren't any bed bugs and somebody else wasn't already in the room, they didn't really seem to care.

The sun was setting by the time we clocked out and said goodbye to Rajat.

We heard wild, idiotic laughter coming from the parking lot. Three guys in their late teens or early twenties were milling around. I knew exactly what was about to happen. One of them had one of those red kickballs I remembered from gym class. They formed a triangle. The one with the ball drew his arm back and launched the ball at one of the other guy's faces. He didn't try to catch it. He just took it, nearly screaming with laughter, before running off to chase the ball. They'd do this until one of them went down. The remaining two would then hurry back to their truck and drive off.

"What the fuck?" Marnie said.

"The Cum Rag Boys," I said.

Marnie looked to Rajat for confirmation.

"The Cum Rag Boys," he said with a nearly wistful smile.

"We'll just stick around here until they're gone," I said. "Usually only takes a few minutes."

As we watched them, I explained the ritual of the Cum Rag Boys. It had been happening nearly weekly for the past few years or so. It was mostly annoying but sometimes broke up the boredom of the day.

They made a few rounds with the ball before one of them finally went down.

"You got the traffic cones?" I asked Rajat.

He pulled the two traffic cones up from beneath the counter as we watched the two remaining guys—one of them with a bloody nose—run for their truck.

Rajat continued to hold the cones, waiting to see if the fallen boy would get right back up or if he needed some time to recuperate. Just as Rajat started walking toward the front door, the guy stood up and went running after the truck. Rajat shrugged and returned the cones.

"How did I not know about this?" Marnie said.

"The mysteries of the Midwest Palms Motel," I muttered.

"You ready?" Marnie said and this simple question plunged me into a near existential quandary. Ready for what? Ready to leave the motel? Ready to have my life completely changed? Ready to go back to my sad house with my sad mom and continue my process of slow rot? So many unanswered questions.

Why did you come back?

Who was that man?

"You okay?" she asked and I realized I never answered her.

After my nervous system kicked me back into the present, I dry swallowed and said, "Sure."

The chirping drone of insects settling down for the day surrounded us as we walked to our cars. There was some commotion from the Cum Rag Boys down by the road. The one who'd fallen was throwing rocks at the truck. It finally stopped and began backing up.

Marnie lit a cigarette and squinted against the sun. "I want you to follow me home."

"Ugh," I said. "I need to go home and shower."

"You're fine," she said.

"If by fine you mean super gross. You didn't *see* the vomit party after-math."

"You know, I *have* a shower."

"And then I'm just going to put my vomity clothes back on?"

She moved closer to me, exhaled a plume of smoke away from my face. "I have a washer and dryer too. Don't tell anyone. That'll just make me look like I'm lazy for wearing the same clothes every day. Speaking of which, I even have clean clothes for you to wear while you wait for yours. I have . . . practically everything."

"I'm still not feeling incentivized."

She flicked her cigarette out in the parking lot, closed the distance between us, pushed me up against my car, and kissed me, her hands touching my sweaty face and tangling in my hair. There was an almost frenzied quality to it I found flattering. I felt something inside of me melt and reach out for her.

Marnie broke away and said, "How bout now?"

"Feeling more incentivized." This might have been the most flirta-tious thing I'd ever said in my life. This was a strange new ritual for me.

"Raj probably has a huge hard-on right now. You know he just sits around watching porn on his laptop all day?"

"I assumed as much. He's always so flustered when I come in there. Harry too. I think they need to get out more."

We both glanced back toward the office to see Rajat standing there, his face practically plastered to the glass.

"Let's take off," Marnie said. "Maybe we can send him a selfie later."

We both got in our cars and drove to Marnie's.

When we got there, a woman with very red hair—presumably her landlord—was watering flowerbeds in the backyard of the house with the few remaining moments of light. Marnie waved to her and the older woman returned the gesture.

So normal, I thought. This woman took care of her house. She probably had a husband who was gainfully employed and living with her. They made extra income by renting property. She was a person who found satisfaction from healthy activities such as tending a garden. I tried not to think of my own mother, probably about this woman's age, sitting on a dirty sofa in a filthy house filled with wall-to-wall junk, chain smoking while she watched TV shows explicitly designed to make the viewer a brain-dead zombie, her hand shaking like clockwork every thirty-two seconds.

I followed Marnie up the stairs to her apartment above the garage.

She unlocked her door and lit a cigarette as soon as she was inside.

I already knew where the bathroom was so she told me where the towels were and said she'd grab me a t-shirt and some shorts.

"You probably don't want to wear my underwear, huh?" she said.

"Maybe that's a little creepy."

"Fair. Okay, well, the shower is pretty self-explanatory."

As I stripped down and got in the shower, cranking it as hot as I could, it dawned on me this was the first time I'd ever taken a shower outside of my house. This made me feel unbelievably childlike, frozen in some state of adolescence I'd been unable to shake.

I grabbed my rancid clothes and carried them out of the steamed-up bathroom.

"Where do you want these?" I said.

Marnie stood from the couch. She'd doffed her basketball shorts and wore just the tank top and a pair of light blue underwear with a rainbow over the crotch.

"I'll take em," she said.

She took a few steps toward the kitchen, opened a pair of wood-slatted folding doors and tossed the clothes in the washer part of the stackable unit. She turned the washer on and repositioned her underwear over her ass with a quick tug.

"I might need a quick shower too," she said. "Help yourself to whatever's in the fridge." She seemed tired, like all the excitement she'd displayed at the motel had drained from her.

She disappeared into the bathroom, leaving the door ajar. I grabbed a plastic cup from one of her cabinets and ran some water from the tap. I would have killed for some coffee but I didn't even see a coffeemaker on the counter. I took the water over to the couch and sat down, fatigue immediately overtaking me. My body felt like it hadn't stopped since I'd come over here last night. Marnie's memorabilia—or whatever you wanted to call it—was still scattered around the small coffee table.

I took a sip of water, listening to the insects and distant frogs from the cracked window above Marnie's sink. I felt clean and comfortable in her baggy t-shirt and shorts and, before I knew it, my eyes were closing themselves and I was drifting off.

I awoke to the sound of her lighting a cigarette. Her hair was gathered into a topknot and she wore only a pair of plain pink underwear and a black sports bra.

"Sorry," I said. "I was so tired."

"It's cool. I'm pretty exhausted too. Wanna go lay down?"

I eyed her. "How much sleep would we be doing?"

She coolly took a drag and slowly exhaled, letting her eyes slowly linger over my body, coming to rest where the voluminous shorts gathered between my legs.

"That's up to you," she said. "You said you'd pay me back for helping you. You're here. That's payment enough. We're square."

I took a drink of water. "I'm nervous."

"You're supposed to be," she said.

I set my glass down and stood up. I walked toward her bedroom, removing my shirt along the way. When I reached her bed, I turned to see her standing in the doorway, leaning against the jamb. I slid the shorts off my hips and let them fall to the floor and she was across the room, pushing me back on the bed. I lost all track of time as she made me feel things I could have never imagined. It felt like she was trying to consume me. I had read about people having orgasms but had never experienced one. If that's what Marnie's mouth and hands had brought me to, I was glad I'd waited this long because, if I'd had one earlier, I didn't see how it would have been possible to think about anything else.

Later, we pulled ourselves up against the headboard in her hot little room. I had the feeling I would never be able to make her feel the things she made me feel. I'd heard about people being a little sad after sex. I'd read somewhere the French referred to it as "la petit mort," the little death. Besides my usual sadness, the only sadness I felt was in not knowing when we'd do this again.

"I feel sticky," I said.

"I feel really good," Marnie said in a sleepy voice, rolling over onto her side and throwing an arm over my stomach.

We continued to lie there for a few minutes, she with her arm across my stomach and one of my hands stroking the fine blond hairs on her forearm. The word "intimacy" came to mind and I wondered if that's what this was, having another person to touch as though you would yourself, and hold, and talk to, to try and decipher their emotional code.

Marnie rolled out of bed and said, "Cigarettes."

I immediately wanted her back. "Relax," I told myself. "She'll be back in less than a minute."

She came back with her pack of cigarettes. She pulled one out and lit it.

"Can I, um, can I get one of those?"

She held the pack out to me. "Damn. I must be better than I thought."

I lit the cigarette like a pro. I'd seen it done enough. The first drag was way more pleasurable than I wanted it to be. I thought people were supposed to cough and gag with their first puff. I thought it was only something people did to fit in or because they thought it was cool.

She put the ashtray between us. I thought about those questions I had for her but didn't think now was the right time to ask them. We smoked in silence.

Then, not caring how amateurish I sounded, I asked her another question, one that seemed more relevant to the situation at hand.

"Did I have one?"

"So . . ."—she crushed out her cigarette—"you've never had an orgasm before?"

"If they feel like that, definitely not."

She put her hand on my thigh. "That, dear, was an orgasm. When you reach the point where you have no control over what's happening. You *have* masturbated, right?"

I don't know why this made me blush. "Well, yeah . . . but it never felt like that."

She slid her hand up my thigh and put it where her mouth had been only moments ago.

"Maybe you just need to practice on someone else."

The cigarette suddenly seemed less interesting. I crushed it out.

"I want to feel your mouth on me," she said.

I picked up the ashtray and put it on the nightstand. She scooted down on the bed and I straddled her hips, feeling powerful. We kissed deeply. When I finally pulled away, she looked me in the eye and said, "I want you to try anything you want."

I did.

FIFTEEN

Marnie woke up as I was getting out of bed to go retrieve my clothes.

"Where ya goin?"

"It's late. I need to get home."

"C'mon. Just stay."

"I can't."

Marnie pulled herself up and flipped on the light. "I want to come with you."

I suppressed a laugh. "Oh, I don't think that's a good idea."

"I want to meet your mom." She looked down at her lap, nervously toying with a string from the sheet.

"What?"

"I think I can get some information from her. I've . . . tried talking to her when she's called the motel but she shuts down. Seems confused."

I wasn't sure how to deal with this. I was immediately drowning in embarrassment more than anger. My house was a trash pit. Maybe that was to be expected since I was a housekeeper and I'd always heard it said that the carpenter has the most dilapidated house on the block and the mechanic's car barely runs.

"When did you talk to Mom?" I felt genuinely on the verge of panic.

"Well, I've *tried* a few times but—"

"A few times?"

I didn't think we'd ever transferred my clothes to the dryer. It didn't matter. I'd wear them soaking wet. I just didn't want to be around her at this exact moment because I felt . . . betrayed.

Marnie was right behind me. She was crying.

"Libby, I didn't . . . I don't want you to think . . ."

"Don't want me to think what? That I'm part of your sick little obsession? That you came back from wherever you've been to your boring little hometown and I just happened to be around for your amusement?" I'd never even talked to my mom like that. It was like nearly thirty years of frustration was breaking. "I'm just a fucking plaything. I was there for my big sister's amusement. I'm there for my mom's amusement and to do the motel's dirty work. And for you I'm just here for you to . . . what? Just remember your past and fuck when you get frustrated enough?"

She backed up from me and collapsed onto a corner at the foot of her bed, her shoulders slumped. "It's not like that at all. I'm trying to help you. You're angry because you've never gotten the answers you wanted."

"And you know what? I'm fine with that. I've . . . made peace with it or whatever."

She looked up to meet my eye. "You are not fine with it. Or you shouldn't be, anyway."

"So you . . . what? Think you're liberating me?"

"I just want to give you answers so you can make your own decisions."

"I don't even know what you're talking about. I'm a big fucking girl. I've been making my own decisions for years."

"Have you?"

"Yes," I said more out of stubbornness than anything else.

"Then I guess I misjudged you."

"What do you mean?"

"I don't know if I would have wanted you so much if I knew you'd *chosen* to live this way."

"Well, I'm sorry I can't afford an apartment above the garage on the nice side of town because, as far as I can see, that's the only thing separating us. Actually, it's not just that. At least I didn't get out and have to come back."

Now she was crying harder, head down, tears splashing onto her thighs. I felt like shit but I also felt powerful. I imagined this was the type of petty meanness a lot of people are able to get out of their systems in their teen years before going off to college and trying to convince the adult world they're not sociopaths.

Marnie wiped the tears from her cheeks and lit a cigarette. She didn't offer me one.

"I'm sorry," she said. "I don't know how to explain it but I feel like it's still possible to find an answer."

I tried to imagine the inside of Marnie's brain. She was as broken as I was for different reasons. I wasn't sure I wanted answers to life's difficult questions. I didn't even think I wanted to ask the questions. I was stained early on, earlier than Marnie, and I thought those stains went all the way to the bone. What happened to my sister made me feel dirty. I thought any type of answers I could get would only make me feel dirtier.

I moved closer to Marnie and she put her hands around my hips and pulled me toward her and kissed just below my bellybutton before pressing her tear-slicked face into my stomach.

My throat clicked as I swallowed. "Are things going to change if you meet her?"

She looked up at me, blinking, her eyes red. "I really don't know."

Her lack of reassurance was the most honest answer she could have given me.

"Why did you come back?"

She crushed out her cigarette and looked at me with bloodshot eyes.

"Do you really want to know?"

Marnie looked so miserable I couldn't really be mad at her. I felt kind of sorry for her.

"I want to know everything about you," I said.

She pulled the sheet up to her chin like a protective shield and part of me dreaded what could potentially come out of her mouth.

"I loved Lauren. We were talking about moving away together when . . . before it happened."

And there it was. My anger didn't build. There wasn't any reason for it to. At that moment, I didn't really feel much of anything. Everything I knew about Marnie, about my *sister*, shattered. I felt deflated. Still naked, I slumped onto the edge of the bed.

"It's okay if you hate me," she said.

"No." I was still trying to process what she said. "I can't hate you. We both lost someone we loved."

She scooted forward and began stroking my back. I wanted to shrug off her touch but I welcomed the comfort it brought me.

"We need to do this for Lauren," Marnie said.

I had no response. I didn't want to think Marnie was manipulating me. I knew what she said wasn't true. Like funerals, the living do nothing for the dead. We do it for ourselves.

After a long, uncomfortable silence, Marnie still rubbing my back, I said, "I want you beside me but I need some time to process this."

"I get it," she said. "It can wait."

SIXTEEN

The radio played while I drove home but I wasn't hearing it. I thought I would spend the drive thinking about Marnie, thinking about us, but I didn't. I was too confused to think about anything. What I was doing but didn't realize I was doing was trying not to think about the future. I hadn't ever been much of a planner. I went to school and, later, work, before going home to Mom. When I wasn't in my room reading books, I was usually in the living room with her, watching whatever she wanted to watch. I couldn't even think of any shows I looked forward to watching. Half the reason I read was to spend hours in the library picking out books. I barely finished any of them.

What I ended up mostly thinking about was Marnie and Lauren. They'd been lovers. Of course I hadn't known. It seemed like there was something there. Something I wasn't seeing. I combed my brain for any memories of Marnie. Maybe there was something but I didn't want to force it. I didn't want to seize on a false memory and let it shade what was happening to me now.

I pulled into the driveway, somewhat surprised Mom wasn't standing at the door. It was after midnight and I hadn't even called to tell her I'd be late. I had to remind myself I was a grown woman.

Approaching the house, I had a distinct feeling something had changed. But it hadn't. Not really. The only thing that had changed was that I now had more knowledge. I could be mad at Marnie for not being upfront with me from the beginning, but then I didn't think I would have ever ended up in her bed. Was that her intent? It seemed ridiculous. No way she came back to seduce the little sister of her teenage lover. Marnie was off but she wasn't psychotic.

As I opened the door, I had a thought that wouldn't last long: the only thing that had actually changed was that Marnie was now a suspect. What if her scrapbook had been what most scrapbooks were—a collection of fond memories? What if it was her way of watching the murder recede further and further from the interest of the public and law enforcement?

But then why would she come back and try to stir things up?

I closed the door behind me and waited for Mom to bellow. She wasn't in bed. I heard the TV in the other room. I was exhausted. I thought about going to my room and going straight to bed but didn't want to doze off only to be awakened by Mom pounding on the door.

When I entered the living room and saw Mom on the couch, I knew something was wrong.

She sat in her customary spot, sunk into the crater created by her bony ass. Her eyes were closed and I'd never seen such a peaceful expression on her face. Her gnarled hands were in her lap, a burned-out cigarette clutched between the middle and index finger of her left hand. Beneath her hands was an old VHS tape. Her hands stayed still.

All the emotions I'd bottled up over the past decade-plus felt like a wave that came crashing down on me. What I ultimately felt was not anything I expected to feel. There was a bit of sadness, but it was hard to feel sad for someone who'd rather have been dead a very long time ago.

The surprising things I felt were fear and freedom.

And . . . overwhelmed. I felt *so* overwhelmed.

I didn't need to touch her. I didn't need to utter her name. I didn't need to hold a mirror under her nose. All I had to do was look at her unmoving right hand. I had no idea what I was supposed to do.

I went to the phone in the kitchen feeling like I was on autopilot. I called Marnie's apartment, thinking it was possible she was asleep and hoping with what little hope I had she wasn't.

She answered on the fourth ring.

"Can you come over?" I didn't realize I was crying.

"Are you okay?"

"Just . . . Can you? It's—"

"I know where it is. I'll be there soon. Whatever it is, don't do anything stupid."

"The door'll be unlocked. Just come in."

I did the stupidest thing I could think of in the moment. After unlocking the door, I sat beside Mom, fished a cigarette from her half-empty pack on the filthy coffee table, and lit up. She didn't smell good. I imagined she had soiled herself. If she still had half a pack of cigarettes, she'd probably been dead since late morning or early afternoon.

Marnie was there before I'd finished the cigarette. She had to have driven really fast.

Or she followed you.

She opened the door. "Lib?"

"In here." My voice was still thick with tears.

Marnie appeared at the entrance to the living room. Even in my current state, I found myself thankful she wasn't scanning the squalid little house.

"Oh god. Is she . . .?"

"She's gone."

"Have you called anyone yet?"

I shook my head.

"I'll do it."

"Just . . . wait."

"We can't just wait."

I plucked the videotape from beneath Mom's hands and rattled it at Marnie.

Marnie's face froze in an expression that might have been shock or surprise but looked a lot like fear.

"Do you think it's a clue?" she said.

I took the final drag of the cigarette, expelling the smoke along with a nervous laugh. "Is this *Scooby-Doo?*"

She rolled her eyes. "Are you okay?"

"I . . . I don't know yet."

She crossed the room and pulled the tape from my hand.

"Been a while since I've seen one of these. Is there a way to watch this?"

Now I wanted her to look around the house, wanted her to see the reality of what my life had been since Lauren's death.

"Does it look like anything's changed in the last decade? Does Mom strike you as the type of person who ever had the money to go digital?" I remembered Dad bringing the little camcorder home from the thrift store, so excited, even though hardly anyone used them even then.

All Marnie had to do was turn and look at the TV. It was still on but I must have turned the volume down after coming home.

"My guess is that if you remove all that trash below the TV, you'll find a VCR. Probably still works."

Marnie went about pulling out handfuls of empty cigarette packs, fast food wrappers, and old shopping bags—mostly vintage—to reveal a VCR I remembered being silver but was now a dull gray.

"Well looky there," she said.

"Hopefully mice haven't chewed through the wires."

"Are you sure you want to watch this?" she said to me over her shoulder.

"It's probably nothing. Might be nice."

She put the tape into the VCR and played around with the TV remote until she found the right setting or channel that showed the tape. She came back to the couch and sat on the opposite side of Mom. She lit a cigarette. I lit another one of Mom's and tried to figure out the timeframe and setting of what I was watching.

Lauren and I were in frame, the camera close up on Lauren. The camera image shuddered and I immediately knew it was Mom filming. Lauren smiled, her teeth straight and white, her cheeks flushed perfectly. This had to have been less than a year before she was killed.

"I should ask you if you're sure *you* want to watch this," I said.

Marnie exhaled and I could tell she was crying. "It's been so long."

On the screen, Lauren said, "Today, I am going to give my little sister, Libby Milligan, a *much* needed makeover."

The camera went to me, sitting at a small table in front of a tri-fold mirror. I turned to the camera and smiled big. I was missing a couple of teeth.

Marnie laugh-sobbed at the sight of me.

I was trying to figure out where we were. It definitely wasn't either of the houses. The window's curtains were open beyond the table and the mirror to show what looked like a parking lot.

Then it hit me.

We were at the Midwest Palms Motel. We'd had to stay there for a week while my dad readied the house for us to move in. It had been a foreclosure—the cheapest house in Hyte—and the previous occupants had trashed the place.

"That's the motel," I mumbled just to be saying something.

"Huh," Marnie said.

As nostalgic as it was, the video was really, really boring. Mom's palsied camerawork made me anxious, waiting for the tremor. You could barely hear anything Lauren said as she did my make-up with the back of her head to the camera. Lauren, who, as far as I knew, never wore make-up, was also not great at applying it. I watched through grainy, faded footage as my innocent ten-year-old face became something in between a clown's and a television prostitute's. We managed to stick it out to the final reveal, Marnie and I sitting on either side of my dead mother and smoking cigarette after cigarette. Where had cigarettes been all my life? I felt like I had discovered one of adulthood's great mysteries.

"It's probably a good thing Lauren didn't want to go into cosmetology," Marnie tried to joke.

As the tape cut to static, the sadness replaced the boredom. "I don't think it would have mattered."

"No. I guess you're right."

Neither one of us said it, but I'm sure we both thought Lauren's murder potentially saved the beauty industry.

I got up from the couch and hit fast forward to make sure there wasn't anything else on the tape.

There wasn't.

SEVENTEEN

Over the next couple of weeks, Marnie was like my knight in shining armor. She called 911 that night, telling them it wasn't really an emergency but she didn't know who else to call. They took their time getting there. I stayed in my room. I couldn't watch. The word that kept coming to mind was "undignified." Mom's whole life had been undignified and I couldn't bear to witness this final exclamation point upon that indignity.

Marnie went with me to fill out all the paperwork. We had her cremated. No urn. No funeral. When they called me to pick up the cremains, I contemplated not bothering but thought that might be the greatest indignity of all.

Marnie helped me clean up the house in between crying jags. She couldn't clean worth a damn but she was pretty good at picking stuff up. It felt like pulling back the sad, dark world that had slowly swallowed Mom over the past decade, excavating depression. It all made me feel so guilty, like I should have tried harder to pull her out of her funk. Then I started to get mad at her. Why should I have been the one to rescue her? Who was there to help me manage *my* grief?

And that's when I felt myself getting closer and closer to Marnie. She was there now. She was there to help get me through this. To listen to me when I needed to talk about anything.

We continued going to our shifts at the motel and everything else faded into the background for those two weeks. She was so exhausted from dealing with the house she stayed over a couple of nights. We were so tired we only fucked a couple times and I thought, if we were to stay together, that was probably more like what it would be years down the road, the trauma bonding shaving off that time.

Once we'd finally done all we could do without buying some paint or hiring a handyman, Marnie said, "You want to come back to my place with me? You have to be sick of being here."

As I was increasingly noticing with Marnie, she was more aware of what I was feeling than I was.

"That . . . I'd like that," I said.

Marnie drove her car. The night was clear and warm and we kept the windows down. She turned the radio to some dark, aggressive music and cranked it up way too loud. It had an oddly calming effect and I found myself wondering what Marnie did back in California. She could have been a detective or a psychopath. It could have been more mundane than that. She could have just been a thirtysomething woman with a shitty job who spent her free time playing internet detective. Maybe she was doing all of this so she could take the results home with her and be celebrated among her nerd friends. I didn't really care. For the first time in my life, it felt like a curtain had been pulled far enough back for me to see a little of what was on the other side. I'd never had any previous interest in pulling back the curtain because I assumed whatever lay on the other side was just more squalor and depression. Now I could see a faint glimmer of sunlight. A future where I wouldn't be a pawn or a servant. A future where I could be an actual adult as in control of my life as much as finances would allow.

When we got to Marnie's, I told her I wanted to give *Twin Peaks* another shot. What I really wanted to do was talk. Talk about her. Ask about her past. Since meeting her, it seemed like everything had been about me or my sister or my mother and then back to me again. I didn't want her to think I was as quietly self-involved as I probably was. But I knew we were both emotionally wrung out.

Why did you come back? Really?

I didn't like the almost combative qualifier I'd added to my obsessive question.

We took a shower together while Marnie heated up a frozen pizza in the oven. Her phone vibrated before we got in the shower. She didn't answer it. We ate the pizza on the couch in front of the TV. We watched a reality show about people from various parts of the country who were trying to get cancer. The subject seemed grim but the tone was light-hearted and almost fun. Marnie's phone vibrated again.

"You gonna get that?" I said.

"Nah."

When we were finished eating, I took our paper plates and threw them into the kitchen trashcan. Marnie's phone was vibrating again when I came back.

"Still not going to answer it?"

"Nope."

"Who keeps calling?" Even a question this basic seemed intrusive.

"It's my mom. I don't like talking to her. She calls too much."

This was the first time I'd heard *anyone* call Marnie.

"You can talk to her if you need to."

"It's nothing important, I'm sure." To change the subject, she leapt up from the couch and grabbed the *Twin Peaks* box set. "You wanna start from the beginning?"

"Sure."

"Probably don't want to get high, huh?"

"I think I'll pass."

Marnie put the first DVD into the player, came back to the couch, and packed her bowl. I hadn't really thought about it, probably because I'd been a million miles away, but I couldn't recall Marnie smoking pot while at my house.

Maybe because I was emotionally numb or now had my mother's death fresher in my memory than Lauren's death, but *Twin Peaks* didn't seem so traumatic this time. It almost seemed therapeutic. I found myself thinking I might watch more TV if it were all like this. Within the time it took to watch it, Marnie's phone vibrated several more times. Eventually, she buried it in the couch cushions and I was sure it rang at least a couple more times after that.

The episode finished and Marnie said, "Better that time?"

"Yeah. I actually liked it a lot."

"Cool. We should start knocking the rest of them out."

She pulled out her phone and rolled her eyes at it.

It was vibrating again.

"Seriously," I said, "answer it. I can find something to do while you talk to her."

"This is bullshit, ma'am," she said to me. She flipped open her phone and said, "What?"

I couldn't hear any specific words coming from the other end but Marnie was quickly up and walking to her bedroom. The only thing I heard her say was "I'm a grown-ass woman" before shutting the door.

I went into the kitchen to get a glass of water. I stared out the window at the house on the property. The windows were all darkened so, naturally, it didn't take me long to imagine a silhouette in one of the upper windows, staring back at me. I took a big drink of water and moved away from the window.

The scrapbook of Lauren still sat on the coffee table. I couldn't bring myself to look at it. It seemed weird that something like that documented a person's death rather than life. How weird would it be if I waited until now to start a scrapbook of my mom? Also, if Marnie really had come back to try and find Lauren's killer, she was doing a terrible job.

Eventually, Marnie came out of her bedroom. She didn't have her phone in her hand and I wondered if that was because she expected another rash of phone calls. Her face was red with rage, quite the accomplishment on her mom's part since she'd smoked at least two bowls over the past couple of hours.

I wasn't going to ask her about the phone call, figuring she'd talk about it if she wanted to. Instead, I asked her something I'd thought about while staring at the closed scrapbook.

"Do you have anything like that from when Lauren was alive?"

Why did you come back? Really?

"I used to have quite a few pictures and things but they've gotten lost along the way." She lit up a cigarette and said, "Oh, wait." Then she dashed off to the bedroom and came back with one of those strips you get from photo booths.

I looked at it, the tears almost immediately blurring my vision. One photo showed them smiling. One photo showed them making goofy faces. The third photo showed them kissing, Marnie holding up a middle finger to the camera.

Marnie looked not much different than she did now. I had half-hoped seeing her from this time period would jar some recollection from me but it didn't. I was sure I'd never seen Marnie until she started working at the motel.

"See, now you know we were together and I'm not making it up."

"I never thought you were making it up." Did I? Did I think she had really just come across the case online and decided to pursue it?

"We really weren't together long enough to have a lot of things like that. Plus, you know, there were only a few people who could know we were a couple."

For some reason, that had never occurred to me.

I didn't know what else to say, so I just said, "I never thought you were lying."

"I know. I'm just . . . distracted."

"You want to talk about it?"

"Not right now. It's . . . a lot."

I put the photos of Marnie and Lauren face down on the scrapbook and wiped the tears from my cheeks.

"We've got plenty of time," I said.

The look in her eye, on her whole face, was the saddest expression I'd ever seen her manifest.

I told myself it was because of everything we'd been going through. We were both just tired and emotional but we would come out of it together.

I never doubted that.

EIGHTEEN

I'd felt weird since Mom died. Weird in a way I hadn't really felt before. It was the way I imagined most people felt when leaving high school and going off to college. Somewhere in between sadness and freedom. I knew my relationship with Mom was a purely co-dependent one. I loved her because she was my mother but, in many ways, I blamed her for not being able to untether myself from this boring ass little town. I realized how unfair this was. I'd always looked at myself as *her* emotional support but, as I cleaned the motel room in the same town I'd lived in my entire life, I realized she was, in a sense, providing emotional support for me too. We never talked about it, but if I'd talked about how much I wanted to leave Hyte and what I would do when I did, she wouldn't have told me not to. She wouldn't have said those were stupid ideas. Deep down, she knew me. She maybe knew me better than I knew myself. She knew I would never leave until somebody dragged me away. What I had been going through since the age of ten, she'd witnessed from a more mature, adult perspective. Had probably even seen the exact same behavior by others who'd gone through similar things. Whereas I matured physically but never really attained enough adult experiences to put the trauma of my past into any type of logical perspective.

I thought about these things as I continued cleaning the room in the late afternoon. I only had a couple more to do after that. Surprisingly, Mom had had a life insurance policy, owned the house, and had a modest-sized savings account. And why wouldn't she? Her disability checks arrived like clockwork to her bank account while I paid for all the food and bills with my absurdly small paycheck. Working at the motel now felt like earning actual money I could spend or save as I pleased. I was no longer working just to keep Mom and I alive. Plus, after thoroughly cleaning that house from top to bottom, cleaning a motel room after someone's single night of reckless abandon seemed like easy work.

I was cleaning a shower when I heard the sounds coming from the other room. For some reason, you could hear sounds in the bathroom better than you could hear them anywhere else. I'm pretty sure it had something to do with the venting or lack of carpet.

It was a Saturday and sounded like the renovation guys were starting early. They were off on Saturday and Sundays. Most of them went home to their families. Some of them stayed at the motel. There was one of those huge interstate truck stops an exit south. They'd go there and prowl for lot lizards. Some poor teenage girl who just wants to get away from her parents all the way up through some late-middle-aged woman who needed money for drugs or couldn't let go of that sense of adventure.

I doubted many of these women realized they were being driven back to more men than they thought. Right now, they sounded like they were in the early stages. I couldn't hear any specific words, just the nervous, trying-too-hard female voice punctuated with raucous male laughter. Because I worked during the day, I felt like I was spared the darker side of this, the moment when the woman realizes no amount of cash is worth doing what she was going to have to do but that it was far too late to back out because the consequences would be even worse.

I worked quickly so I could get out of there. This wasn't a rare occurrence but I still felt raw and it hit me in a different way than it normally did. The helplessness of it all. Obviously, what they were doing was illegal, although I'm sure they were well versed on the loopholes to get out of it if anyone ever reported them, which, of course, never happened because those traveling, long-term construction crews were our bread and butter. We had to treat them like a fancy Las Vegas hotel treats celebrities. Let them do whatever they want so the motel keeps getting their money. And, since this crew was renovating the actual motel, it made the situation even more sensitive. I usually managed to forget about it by telling myself these women had to at least be jaded enough to know what they were getting themselves into and there was no rescuing, no saving somebody like that. They would take all they could and quit doing it or desperately keep getting into worse and worse situations.

My thoughts ran away with me as I finished cleaning the bathroom in a near frenzy. I kept thinking about that angry guy handing Marnie money and wondered what I would do if that were Marnie in the next room.

As soon as I finished the bathroom and moved through the sweltering heat to my next to last room, I couldn't hear what was going on in there anymore, but I couldn't stop thinking about Marnie. If it were her, I would be very worried. I wondered if I would stay with her if that's how she chose to make extra money. I'd probably still be her friend but I wasn't sure if I could keep sleeping with her. Maybe I was judgmental. I didn't really see myself as a jealous person.

I rushed through the last two rooms, tucked my cart into the housekeeping closet, and went to clock out and say bye to Marnie, the absurdity of my prior thoughts making me feel like an idiot. Why did I let myself get so worked up about even exploring the possibility the woman in the other room could be Marnie when I could have just stopped by the front desk and put all of my suspicions to rest?

Then I had to ask myself why Marnie hadn't checked in with me all day. She almost always stopped by on at least one of her multiple smoke breaks. It was so hot, I told myself she didn't want to spend the extra time outside trying to find out what room I was working in.

One of my questions was answered when I walked into the front office to see Rajat behind the counter. My crackpot suspicions, on the other hand, went off the radar. I was about to do something I'd never done before and just the thought of it sucked all the moisture from my mouth and sent such an adrenaline rush through me that my hands were shaking so badly I had a hard time clocking out.

"Marnie call in today?" My voice shook even though I tried my hardest to sound casual.

Rajat shrugged. "No call, no show. Trying not to let Dad know so he doesn't fire her."

"I'll talk to her," I managed to squeak out. Lying was even more difficult when you felt like you had zero control over your body. Even though I'd already clocked out, I had to pretend I'd forgotten something. I found the cabinet with the spare towels and washcloths and said, "Totally slipped my mind. The guys in Room 12 asked for some extra towels." I grabbed a couple towels and washcloths. "I'll run them down there before I take off."

"Oh . . . thanks," Rajat said. I had no idea how I must have appeared to him. I felt squirrelly and psychotic.

"See ya Monday," I said.

Before I got back to the door, Rajat said, "I'm sorry about your Mom."

I wanted to turn back around and tell him he'd told me that every day we'd worked together since Mom died and that if he was really sorry he should have convinced his dad to give me some paid time off but I was so nervous I felt like puking so I just mumbled "Thanks," the only thing I was capable of, before leaving the office and entering the afternoon heat.

I began walking toward Room 12, where the "party" was taking place. I had to do it fast or I wouldn't do it at all.

I knocked on the door. They would expect people to be coming and going all night long, so I knew they wouldn't even ask who it was before opening the door.

An overweight middle-aged guy wearing a Miller High Life promotional t-shirt opened the door, unleashing a wave of cigarette smoke and alcohol fumes.

"Yeah?" he said.

"I . . . have your towels." I'd nearly forgotten they'd never asked for towels and was genuinely surprised when he turned to the others in the room and asked if anyone had requested towels.

My panicked search of the room yielded instant results. There were a couple more guys sitting on the beds in the room. They looked the same as the guy who'd opened the door. The desk the TV sat on was covered in bottles of booze and, standing in front of the TV was a woman . . . who was as not-Marnie as you could possibly get. I did feel sorry for her but she looked pretty seasoned and I was just relieved it wasn't Marnie, both for her and me.

"Hello?" the guy at the door said and I realized I'd completely missed him saying they hadn't requested towels.

I had the completely irrational fear of him grabbing me and dragging me into the room and something in my brain short circuited.

I held out the towels and said, "Towels," almost yelled it, and he took them out of a surprised kind of obligation and I turned and walked to the parking lot at a quick pace.

"You can bring that ass back to the party any time," he called after me and all my panicked suspicions melted into a more status quo form of self-loathing and feeling like an idiot in general.

I got in my car and considered driving by Marnie's before going home but I didn't want to seem too possessive, especially after my imaginative gymnastics of the last couple hours.

NINETEEN

I drove through a fast-food place on the way home. I set the bag on the kitchen table you wouldn't have been able to see three weeks ago. I called Marnie. She didn't answer. I was too upset to eat so I put the bag of food in the refrigerator that was, for the first time ever, filled only with the stuff I ate and drank. It was an extremely selfish thought but I realized just how alone I would be if anything happened to Marnie. What if she'd decided to leave and go back to California? Why didn't she ever talk about her life there?

Why did you come back? Really?

I couldn't keep thinking about this. I'd felt off since hearing those men in the other room. That was magnified by Marnie's absence at the motel. I felt dirty, like I'd done something wrong. I felt guilty for allowing myself to think we had any future whatsoever. If not guilty, then at least presumptuous. Who'd want to spend the rest of her life with me?

I decided to take a shower, something I did most days after working at the motel. In the shower, I kept thinking of those men. It didn't really make any sense. Marnie taking money from one of the older ones was what really bothered me. That, somehow, there was a connection there.

I got out of the shower and tried Marnie again. Still no answer.

I went into the living room and sat on the couch. As far as I knew, the

VHS tape of Lauren and I was still in the VCR. There was something about that I thought I was missing too. Maybe it was because I hadn't had the chance to watch it alone. Would that help me process it any better? Was there anything to process? I was sure Mom had a lot of tapes of us. Marnie and I hadn't touched the basement yet. Why would Mom have chosen that one at that exact moment? It wasn't like she was going to watch it. She wanted me to find it. She wanted me to watch it.

I picked up the remote control, rewound the tape to the beginning, and hit play.

I was, obviously, watching the same thing I'd watched a few weeks ago with Marnie. What had I not seen or heard when we watched it together? There was me, sitting at the desk in front of the mirror, Lauren turned toward the camera. I let my gaze go to the window, out into the parking lot. There was a black truck more or less centered in the frame of the window. Another truck to its left. A smaller car to the right. I waited for Mom to move the camera toward me. I could now make out a logo on the tailgate of the pickup. The quality of the tape was too compromised for me to read it, and maybe I was making something out of nothing, but the logo seemed familiar. I would have bet anything, if I *could* have made out what it said, it would read "Seabliss Renovation Company."

Seabliss was a local company. I'd seen their trucks around town for years. For a project like the one at the motel, they brought in additional contractors from the outside. There was something about that connection that didn't sit right with me. Again, I didn't know if it was the connection to Marnie or something else. That was probably the last time the motel had been renovated. Now they were renovating it again and Marnie just happened to be back in Hyte. It probably meant nothing. Then I couldn't stop thinking of passing the rooms they were renovating—the plastic tarps covering the floors, the lecherous catcalls and sometimes vulgar hooting. But most of the workers were younger than me . . . Except for what I thought of as the boss, the older guy I'd seen with Marnie.

I started feeling overly paranoid. Did Marnie never talk about her past because she would have had to lie about it? I let it slide, but she'd lied about her connection to Lauren at first, pretending she'd merely been obsessed with the case in high school and waiting to tell me they were lovers. Did I suspect Marnie had something to do with Lauren's death? Wouldn't that be perfect? I had no idea what that kind of love was like, but if it existed, my feelings toward Marnie were the closest I'd ever gotten. Was I looking for some obstacle to make it impossible to come to fruition?

I let the tape play out, so fixated on that truck in the parking lot I couldn't really pay attention to anything else. I became more and more anxious.

I tried calling Marnie again and didn't get an answer.

After hanging up the phone, I stood there, knowing I was going to go to Marnie's even if it made me seem like a jealous, overbearing cunt.

Even though the sun was low in the sky, it was still unbearably hot out, the air hazy enough to give everything a soft focus. There were still a couple packs of Mom's cigarettes in the glove compartment. I grabbed one of the packs, ripped it open, and depressed the dash lighter, something I hadn't used since taking the car over from Mom. I took a drag of the cigarette and had the most out-of-place thought that I probably needed to get the registration switched over at some point.

Where were you on that one, Marnie?

I pulled out of the drive and onto the road, my nerves as skittish as the bugs bouncing off my windshield. I was anxious but, deep down, I knew there was probably a very simple explanation for Marnie's absence. Maybe she had something better to do. Maybe she actually was sick and didn't feel like answering her phone. I just hoped she would at least be home so I could put my fears to rest. Not to mention that I wanted to see her. This was the longest we'd been apart since first hooking up.

What if she just needed a break?

Then we could talk about it. We probably needed to talk about some things anyway.

Why did you come back? Really?

Who was that man and why was he giving you money?

I turned into Marnie's driveway. The landlady was once again in the flowerbeds, this time at the front of the house. What had seemed comfortingly mundane previously now seemed slightly psychotic given the excessive heat and the frantic vigor with which the woman went about her weeding. I couldn't really take my eyes off her until I was past the house and she was out of eyesight. There was no polite wave this time. Oddly, watching someone so feverishly obsessed with aesthetics did something to lighten my mood. Or maybe it was the sight of Marnie's car in its usual spot. By the time I put my car in park and got out, my sense of dread had lifted somewhat.

Luckily, my self-loathing and anxiety had many levels so I came back to the one where I was being a jealous, overprotective cunt but went ahead with what I was going to do because I figured Marnie needed to see this side of me too.

I took the steep wooden steps up to Marnie's door. When she came to my house, she just came right in. I thought about doing that but didn't want to go too far. I knocked on the door. I strained to hear movement—anything, even the sound of a TV—coming from inside. I was so focused on that I didn't hear the landlady shuffling around my car and approaching the steps. I was going to ask her if she knew where Marnie was when the door opened.

Marnie stood there in her sports bra and basketball shorts looking like all the life had been sucked out of her.

I wanted to ask her why the fuck she couldn't answer her phone but she spoke before I could.

She said, "You shouldn't have come here."

Immediately after that, something very hard hit the side of my head. My hand went to the spot as I collapsed against the railing. Marnie came out of her apartment.

"No!" she said just as another hard thing hit me in the back of the head.

Christ, I was getting stoned. I heard Marnie start down the steps and had an insane image of the landlady chucking rocks she'd pulled from the garden at my head.

But why? was my last thought before a much larger one hit me in the forehead and everything went black.

TWENTY

When I finally came to, everything seemed very far away. It wasn't like waking up. It was like immediately resuming the panic I felt after getting hit with the first rock. My head throbbed with pressure but the rush of adrenaline kept the pain at bay. I was thankful for that.

The woman who'd hit me with the rock stood over me. I now had no idea how I'd ever considered her remotely normal. Her fire engine-red wig was askew. The make-up she wore looked deranged but I didn't know if that was how she applied it or if it was from the exertion of slinging rocks at my head and then pulling me inside. There was something familiar about her but that might have been because I'd seen her around town. There was no sign of Marnie.

I was on the floor of Marnie's apartment, somewhere between the coffee table and the TV. The coffee table had been tipped over and shoved against the couch. I was completely naked, my arms tied above my head. When I tried moving my arms, it was met with resistance so I assumed I was tethered to something. I looked down at myself and saw that my ankles were separated by a woodblock. I felt completely humiliated and exposed.

"Look who's all bright eyed now," the woman said. I immediately regretted opening my eyes. My mouth felt dry and swollen but I wasn't planning on saying anything anyway. The woman pressed the toe of her shoe against my pubic hair and said, "What is it about you Milligan girls' pussies my daughter finds so compelling? She just can't stay away, I guess."

I should have been trying to think of how to get away but what the woman said turned me completely upside down. It was like almost everything clicked into place. If this was Marnie's mother, I was willing to bet the man I'd seen at the motel was her father. Her apartment was above their garage and I felt certain that if I were to look in that garage, I'd see that black truck with the Seabliss Renovation Company logo on the tailgate.

She kept her toe pressed between my legs, now grinding her shoe, twisting and pulling my pubic hair. I was aware of the pressure but not the pain. My heart raced and my head swam. I felt like I could lose consciousness at any moment.

"I didn't know you was workin at that motel," she said. "Now I know why Marn felt like gettin out and gettin a job was so important. Almost like she could smell it. Good thing you're the last one. I can get this taken care of and we can finally get on with our lives. It's a good thing your mom died so I don't have to worry about my baby sniffin after that dried up old thing."

I used what little strength I had to pull on the rope binding my wrists. Having been in Marnie's apartment a few times, I doubted there was anything that couldn't be pulled over or apart with a little bit of muscle.

I stared at the woman as she circled around me, following her with my eyes and nearly making myself dizzy in the process. I was trying to catch her eye. How could someone who raised a daughter not have at least a shred of empathy for someone else's daughter? But she was gone. The couple times I managed to make eye contact with her only reaffirmed how serious my troubles were. It was that gone look you see in the eyes of the politically brainwashed, the delusional, the unreasonably fervent.

And I was wrong about thinking I was someone else's daughter. I wasn't. Not anymore. To this woman, I was the end. I was the loose end. I could be wrapped in plastic and dragged into the woods or into a cornfield to be discovered during harvest season. No one would miss me. Maybe Rajat's family would, but they thought I was strange anyway and, after a few unanswered phone calls, they'd just tell themselves they knew I'd stop coming sooner or later and hire somebody else.

"Marnie never knew it was me that took care of Lauren. I think that was a failure on my part. This time, I'm not gonna be so quick. I think it's time she learn that her actions impact other people. Rip them completely apart. Eventually I'll have to get rid of you, but I want her to know you're close, you're right here, but completely useless for her carnal needs."

She grabbed something from the TV stand. She fooled around with it and I could tell what it was by the sound before I ever saw the flame.

A blowtorch.

The fear went beyond paralyzing and into blind panic. I now knew why my legs were pulled apart, cunt exposed. I imagined all my nerves as rubber bands stretched to their breaking point. I began screaming, kicking my arms and legs, trying to create some violent storm to keep this woman away from me.

With the blowtorch in one hand, she raised her foot and brought it down into the middle of my stomach. She did this again and again until I stopped thrashing and turned my head to throw up. She kicked me in the mouth. If my head didn't already feel like it was filled with cotton, this would have hurt a lot.

"You best just lay there and let me do what I need to do," she said.

Because of the ropes, my movement was limited anyway. All I could do was writhe with the discomfort in my stomach.

She stepped in between my calves. If I had some way to push her back, she'd trip over the wood between my ankles and go sprawling but I didn't see how that would be possible.

"The problem with this world is that there are too many sluts in it." She bent over with the torch.

She touched the torch to my pubes, sending a sharp pain through my groin as the room filled with the acrid stench of burning hair. I almost threw up again.

"Smell that, Marn?" She cocked her head up, resembling a feral animal, the torch so close to my stomach I could feel its heat.

She had her free hand between my legs, opening me, sticking her fingers up into me.

"I'm gonna burn you up from the inside out."

I tried to let my mind go. I wanted to be anywhere other than here, even if only mentally. Since I'd never been in a position where I might die, I thought this might be normal. All I could think about was Marnie. Marnie, having to grow up with this woman. Marnie, who, after tonight, would exist in a world with this woman and without me. And how this woman would keep on living, whether she was caught or not, while my sister, mother, and I would exist only as ash.

She got down low on her knees like she was trying to look inside me.

I felt the intense heat between my legs. Something inside of me broke and shut down. I'm not sure my body relaxed as much as I simply tried to dissociate myself from it to minimize the impending pain.

It never came.

Just as I was sure the flame had made contact with my flesh, the woman was suddenly moving away from me. I thought it was possibly my body moving toward death until I saw Marnie standing over top of her, pulling her back, an arm around her neck. The torch hit the floor right next to me and Marnie kicked it away.

I could not raise my head enough to see the woman. I could see Marnie's head, the hair soaked with blood, and her arm as she raised a hunting knife and plunged it down again and again and again. She didn't stop until her arm was painted red.

She moved closer to me, standing over me, and I knew something wasn't right and hoped it was because of the angle. She stood but she was crooked, like she had been frozen in the process of turning to crack her back.

She dropped to her knees and cut the rope from my wrists.

She handed me the knife and said, "You'll have to get the rest."

She vomited as I sat up, my consciousness swimming, before hacking at the ropes binding my ankles.

I could smell the smoke and the only thing I could think about was getting out of there and trying not to pass out. I kicked the wood block and stood up with greater ease than I would have thought.

Marnie was still on the floor, trying to stand up. It looked like only half her body was working.

"We need to get out of here." I lowered myself beside her, threw one of her arms over my shoulders and stood us both up.

As we began hobbling toward the front door, I made it a point to look at Marnie's mother, her corpse bathed in red, the clothes she'd been wearing now punctured with what looked like a hundred slits.

I got Marnie to the door and when I pulled it open and helped her outside, I'd never smelled air that fresh, even though it was probably the hottest night of the year and there was no trace of a breeze.

I managed to practically carry Marnie down the stairs and we scraped our way across the cement driveway and over to the lawn where I sat her down as gently as possible before collapsing next to her.

I pulled her close to me and we watched the garage burn. I imagined her mother screaming in there even though I knew she was dead.

Who was this person I held in my arms?

Marnie mumbled something like "I wanted to tell you . . ." and I found myself waiting for something else.

Why did you come back? Really? Did you come back? Did you ever leave?

I had so many questions for Marnie. Questions that would never be asked. Questions that would never be answered.

As I heard the sirens start up in town, I knew I'd already lost her.

KILL

YOUR

NEIGHBOR

ONE

The cul-de-sac was quiet. The inside of my head was not. I looked over at Emma, hoping she could restore some sense of calm, but she was flushed and breathing heavily—almost panting—her eyes wide, the machete clutched in her right hand. Under the faint moonlight, she glowed with a feverish excitement.

"Emma . . ." I didn't even know what else I'd planned to say.

"You're not backing out now, Kip," she said through clenched teeth. She never used my name. This was serious.

I clutched the butcher knife tighter, as if to draw some steely resolve from its cold metal blade.

"No. Of course not, dear." My voice shook and quavered around the tightness in my chest.

We crossed into Meg Chinaski's yard for the first time since we'd moved next door nearly two years ago and it felt like entering some hostile enemy territory. The amount of bullying and harassment she'd subjected us to in that time period carried a palpable weight. Her weapon was her very presence.

Emma and I were not hotheads. We were not savages. We were not fighters. The list of offenses that took us into our neighbor's yard that night was long. They were little things that added up. Perhaps we could have filed suit against her on a couple of the offenses but, with the purchase and moderate fixing up of the house, we didn't have any money for a lawyer. Even if we did have the money, we wouldn't have had the time. We were busy people.

Do you know who wasn't a busy person?

Meg Chinaski.

And that made her devious evil seem almost insurmountable.

She had one of the most valuable resources when it came to fighting a long, quiet war: time.

Of course, given the fact she was almost permanently tethered to three yapping dogs meant even the quiet war was never really that quiet.

Ultimately, this was the only solution Emma and myself could think of. And, okay, maybe things had grown a little stale between us. And, okay, maybe it was mostly Emma's idea.

TWO

While Chinaski may have had all the time in the world, one thing she didn't have was money. That much was clear and it was going to work against her now. She didn't even have a porch light and, since we'd turned ours off and the streetlight had been out since we moved here, her yard was dark, dark, dark.

It would have been easier to just hop the fence into her backyard but one of the previous owners had erected a twelve-foot-high privacy fence between the two backyards.

So we quickly crossed the front yard, not even watching out for the copious piles of dog shit landmining the overgrown lawn. By the time we reached the far side of her house and the gate leading into the back-yard, we were cloaked in a cloud of feces.

No lock on the gate.

No motion sensitive lights.

Too poor.

The constant roar of Chinaski's air conditioner completely hushed the slightest sounds of our actions.

I started to round the back corner of the house and Emma gripped my wrist with a latex-gloved hand.

"Wait," she said.

This still didn't feel real to me. I just wanted to charge in and get it done or, better yet, get really close to actually doing it and then chickening out. Going back to the way things were. Taking the time to come up with a more logical, less homicidal, and way less illegal plan.

I turned to Emma, looked into her wild, beautiful eyes. "What is it?"

"Kiss me," she said.

I swallowed hard. My mouth was dry. My nervous system felt overloaded and I shook like I had some kind of palsy.

One hand still holding the machete, she overlaid her wrists at the back of my neck and rose to her tiptoes as she pulled me down and into her. It was nearly impossible to respond. Her lips suctioned against mine and her fat wet tongue probed around in my dry cavity, but all I could think about was the pervasive stench of dog shit and the roar of the air conditioner and what we were about to do.

I tried to think of other things. The stars and moon overhead. The sweet smell of fresh cut hay in the distance and the woods behind the cul-de-sac. Emma's perfect face and lithe little body. The confidence and power radiating from within her.

But the nervous fear felt impenetrable and she broke the kiss and shrank back into herself.

"I'm not doing this alone," she said.

When it came to buying the house, we didn't do our proper research. We did the basic research. The house was structurally sound. Newer roof. Newer a/c unit and water heater. No mold. All we'd really have to do was slap some paint on the walls inside and take up the carpet to reveal the original oak floors and we'd be good for a while. The asking price was comparable to other houses in the area. So, on paper, everything looked great. But we had a time crunch. Our current lease was up in a couple of months and the landlord didn't offer any month-to-month terms. So it was either lock ourselves into another year of rent we could barely afford or bite the bullet and try for an affordable mortgage in a less desirable area.

We asked to see the house on Hooper Court two minutes after the realtor sent us the listing.

I was at Broagies, unwinding from the lunch rush, when Emma texted the listing to me.

"Whaddya think?" the text accompanying the listing said.

"Hooper Court makes me think of basketball," I texted back.

"We're meeting the realtor at 5:30."

"OK."

I fired up the ancient PC on my desk and pulled up the listing. It was a two-bedroom Cape Cod. Exactly what we wanted. Less housework and lower heating and air-conditioning bills. It was one of only four houses on the cul-de-sac and there was a nature preserve behind it and, behind that, something called Point Park. I had to research that to make sure it wasn't a shooting range or a kennel or motorcycle club or something. It turned out to be a type of country club, private, exclusively for executives of The Point, a ubiquitous chemical/ defense/ pharmaceutical/ medical/ food company. Emma worked for them in Human Resources. I wondered if she'd ever been to Point Park.

I looked at the ten or so images of the place and tried not to get my hopes up. It seemed like everything we'd looked at that was remotely in our price range had been previously occupied by a pack of wild animals who never took off their shoes and didn't mind if their dogs and cats just shat on the floors.

"Checked it out. Looks good," I texted Emma.

There was a light knock on the office door.

"It's open," I said.

The door opened and Chloe Brenner peered timidly into the office.

"Mr. Dupree?" she said.

"Yeah?" I wasn't going to ask her to call me Kip again.

"I gotta take off. Remember? I've had this abortion scheduled for like a week." She rolled her eyes.

"Yeah. I'm on my way up."

I stood and followed her to the counter, watching the way the black uniform pants hugged her tight, teenage ass. It was nice, but Emma's was better.

The front door jangled and we both turned to the morbidly obese middle-aged couple entering the store and said, as loud as we could, "Welcome to Broagies! Where the fist bumps are always free!"

Chloe took off her hat and exited the store.

I pulled a sheet of butcher paper from the spool, slapped it down on the counter, tried not to acknowledge the growths on the man's face, and asked, "How hard do you want to bro today?"

Then I reached my fist over the glass and he dazedly bumped it and I smiled as big as I possibly could and slid my hands into some disposable plastic gloves.

Emma picked me up after work and we drove to the house at 6 Hooper Court. The day was overcast and most of the neighborhoods we drove through to get there were depressing but nearly every neighborhood in this area was depressing and we were pretty familiar with the area so it wasn't a big shock. The cul-de-sac was at the end of a particularly distressed neighborhood but seemed somewhat dislocated from it. The house we would be looking at sat at the end of the cul-de-sac and almost gave the impression of being surrounded by woods. It wasn't the Twin Springs retreat we both dreamed of but it seemed like we could almost delude ourselves into thinking it was.

Our realtor, Jim Hagathorne, wasn't there yet so we pulled into the driveway and got out.

Emma's mouth ticked up into a smile.

"Pretty quiet," she said.

"Yeah." Other than the distant hum of the highway and the chirping insects and birds, it was, oddly, pretty quiet. Of course, we'd been living in an apartment downtown so just about any place would have been quieter than that.

We looked around at the other houses on the cul-de-sac. The two on the ends looked vacant. No lights. No cars in the driveway. Lawns wildly overgrown. Flowerbeds full of weeds.

The house to the left of the one we were looking at (I had to fight the urge to think of it as ours) actually looked worse than the possibly vacant houses but there were signs of life, however sad that implied life might be. The yard was actually the most overgrown one and the flowerbeds were not just in need of weeding, they looked like they contained nothing but weeds. A red SUV was parked in the unpaved driveway and had the appearance of not moving very much. The grass and weeds growing up through the gravel didn't even look mashed down. All the houses were the same white Cape Cod style but this one was covered in a layer of black mold that had turned it gray.

I come from a long line of white trash and, after living downtown and watching people harvest cigarette butts from public ashtrays, scrounge for food and beverages from trashcans, and piss in the open, the state of the neighboring property wasn't cause for major alarm. I was comfortable with—sometimes even thought I might prefer—trashiness. My biggest cause for concern was the two dogs staring out the bay window and yapping. They were not big dogs. But, still, they were dogs.

Emma noticed them too. "I hope that's not a problem," she said.

"There's not going to be any getting away from dogs in this area."

She sighed. "I know."

Emma and I were both basically vegetarians for ethical as much as health reasons, so it wasn't like we hated dogs or animals. We would have probably had cats if I weren't deathly allergic. In the last few years of living in the apartment, we'd had a series of people living across the hall from us, all of whom owned dogs, and all of those dogs seemed to bark nearly non-stop. The first time around we'd called the police to lodge a noise complaint. The police came. The barking quieted for a day or two. And then the next time Emma and I had anyone over or the TV up too loud after ten p.m., there would be a cop knocking on the door saying they'd received a noise complaint about us. There was no winning. I could have gone into a philosophical debate with the officer. About how there are human sounds and animal sounds. Humans will have friends, they will laugh and carry on, they will raise their voices in joy and anger, they will watch TV and listen to music, sometimes too loudly, because these things are basic human nature. Unless one is blind, there is no necessity in owning a dog. The sound of a dog barking is the animal world intruding into the civilized world, which is fine in the wilderness, but not in an urban apartment where you're paying more than a thousand dollars a month to live. It is up to the humans to keep the animals at bay. One could argue and say it's all the animal world and we invaded it but I don't see dogs being smart enough to build roads and houses. Anyway, it's ultimately never about the dogs, it's about the owners.

We began walking around the house, making sure there weren't any cracks or holes, that none of the windows were busted out, that scrappers hadn't made off with the a/c unit.

"Looks pretty good," Emma said as we rounded the back corner of the house.

Attached to the back of the house was what I thought was the crown jewel—a redwood deck, screened in and covered. I could immediately see us sitting there on summer evenings, having drinks and listening to insect sounds as dusk dropped onto the woods out behind the backyard.

I stood in the middle of the deck and said, "From right here, you can't see a single other house."

Emma smiled again and I could tell she was fighting off an even bigger smile, not wanting to get too excited, girding herself against almost inevitable disappointment.

"Yeah," she said. "It's nice."

And between us, there was that unspoken thing we'd already gone through a couple of times. Like with the house by the cemetery. Or the one surrounded by cornfields. They had been in our price range. We'd fallen in love with them. We'd already pictured ourselves living there. And they were both already gone by the time we made the offer. Were probably even gone before we looked at them. But we'd had a different realtor then and had to let him go. Maybe Hagathorne would come through for us.

We heard the crunch of his tires in the driveway and went around to meet him.

I grabbed a bag out of our car and said, "Hey, man, I brought you a broagie!" and handed it to him before he could even get out of the car.

THREE

On one of my previous lawn mowing sessions, I'd grabbed a couple bricks that were part of the retaining wall for one of our backyard flowerbeds and, careful to make sure Chinaski wasn't in her backyard, flung them over the high privacy fence. The likelihood of her discovering them before we did our deed was slim. Of course, I was hoping the deed would go undone. I was hoping we'd never find ourselves in her backyard searching for those bricks.

Yet, here we were.

"Use the light on your phone," Emma said.

Back here, we were even closer to the outdated air-conditioning unit and its roar muffled Emma's words.

"Huh?" I said.

"Your phone. Use your phone."

I reached into my pocket with my free hand, trying to keep the shaking under control. I pressed the button to activate the screen, not knowing if it would react to my touch through the latex gloves. My hands shook so badly I kept pressing the wrong app.

Frustrated, Emma snatched the phone from my hand and said, "I'll do it."

She quickly turned the flashlight on and went walking deeper into the backyard.

Chinaski didn't seem to have any discernible schedule so there was no guarantee she was snoozing away in her bed. I glanced toward her gross house, half expecting to see her peering out through a parted blind. But there weren't even any lights on.

I heard Emma say something and began walking toward her.

"What?" I asked.

"I said I can't carry both of them."

I drew up next to her and she handed my phone back to me. I pocketed it and we both bent down to pick up one of the bricks.

"We're going to try the back door first, right?" I said.

"I guess," Emma practically huffed.

We'd discussed this previously. Obviously, if the back door were unlocked, our entrance would be much quieter. Emma had argued against it, saying it didn't matter. The dogs would start going crazy as soon as they heard the door anyway. Also, we were both pretty sure Chinaski was a paranoid schizophrenic and didn't think she'd ever leave her doors unlocked. Probably afraid everyone was after her shitty, moldy hoard. My winning rationale was that it would simply be a lot safer to walk in through a door if we didn't have to compete with shards of broken glass. I got the feeling that Emma wanted the explosion of sound, the chaos.

I glanced over at her, beautiful in the moonlight, and thought about saying, "Can't we just go home?"

But I didn't.

She began walking toward the house and I followed her.

"That was quite a welcome to the neighborhood, huh?" Emma said.

We lay in bed on our first night in our new house.

"I'm sure she's harmless," I said. "Maybe just not very friendly."

"Or she's zonked on meds."

Once the movers had moved everything into the house, we'd gone downtown to grab some falafel and fries from the Middle Eastern place.

The neighbor was out. It was the first time we'd seen her. At that point, we weren't even sure it was just her living there. She stood in the front yard, three small dogs restrained by leashes and yapping about two feet from our driveway. I don't really like to immediately profile people but, at first sight, I classified her as straight up white trash. I like to think I know where I come from. She had the kind of pinched, clueless yet angry face so many people in this part of the country seem to wear constantly. Her hair was gray and greasy and matted. She wore a heavily stained plain blue t-shirt that I guessed was about a 4X, sad gray sweat pants, and plain white tennis shoes. It made me think she just went to the dollar store and grabbed the first and biggest things she saw. Were it not for her massive, unrestrained breasts, I would have had no idea if she were a man or a woman.

I grabbed our bag of food and stepped out of the driver's side.

She approached me.

Rather, it was like she was pulled along by the dogs approaching me, gnashing their little teeth and barking furiously with a high pitch that stabbed me somewhere in the back of my brain, lighting some kind of rage center that sent my adrenaline shooting off the charts.

"How ya doin?" I looked at her mottled, cheese-like face. Tried to make eye contact but she just stared wild-eyed at her furiously barking dogs.

I assumed the bag of food was what the dogs were barking at so I just hoisted it up and said, more or less shouting to be heard over the dogs at this point, "Falafel and fries!"

Still getting no response, I just shrugged my shoulders, said, "Nice meeting you too," and turned toward the house.

Emma was already unlocking the door.

I followed her in and turned the lock behind us.

Emma laughed.

"What's so funny?" I asked. "That was horrific."

"Do you think that crazy bitch even knows what falafel is? She probably thinks you were making fun of her."

"You're right. I probably should have just told her it was filled with bombs and liberal ideology."

"Christ. Welcome to Trumpland, I guess."

"Maybe it won't be that bad." I parted the blinds to our front window to see if she was still out there. She was. "I'm pretty sure the dogs are pissing on the car's tires."

Without any words being exchanged between the neighbor and us, the mild irritation deepened to a low-level hate over the next few weeks.

We would be sitting in our living room, trying to read or watch movies, and the sonic landscape would be torn asunder by the yapping of the dogs. It was clear she was walking them over to the extreme edge of her property, putting them as close to us as possible.

"You know," I said, "you would think she'd take them to the other side of the yard if they're going to bark like that. I don't think anyone lives over there. Or just let them run around in the backyard. It's fenced."

"She's just a psycho cunt," Emma said. "She's trying to bother us. She thinks we're like her and she wants a fight. She wants one of us to go out there raging."

More often than not, the neighbor would be standing in her yard with one-to-three dogs, always approaching us and barking furiously, when we came and went. We still hadn't bothered doing any research on her so we began making suppositions based on casual observations.

She didn't work. We'd never seen her SUV leave the driveway. Maybe she no longer drove. She was older, so she could be retired. But she also looked borderline homeless and seemed wildly unstable so it was just as likely she was on some sort of disability.

We'd never seen anyone else come or go from the house so were pretty sure she lived alone.

For the first couple of weeks, if we saw her out there, we'd wave and say hi, but quickly abandoned that practice when all we got were blank stares and angry barks.

So, instead, we just started making medical assessments of her.

"Maybe she'll die soon," I said.

"She doesn't look very good," Emma said.

"Morbidly obese for sure. Her heart could just give out in her sleep."

"She was wearing shorts yesterday. She had a nasty looking rash on her leg."

"Hm. Probably has diabetes."

"I heard her out with her dogs again last night. Sounded like she was about to hack up a lung."

"With the way that air conditioner runs, she probably has Legionnaire's or something."

We tried telling ourselves she was just a nosey, lonely old lady quite possibly in the early stages of Alzheimer's or just had a weak brain partially rotted by years of a poor diet and little to no exercise.

Until we started noticing the shit.

Piles of it everywhere.

The dogs were tiny, so it wasn't like the piles were massive, but they seemed to be strategically placed all along our driveway and even the strip between the sidewalk and the road. We only had the one car so we never parked on the street, but I guess she wanted to cover all of her bases.

"Isn't there a law that says you have to pick up after your animals or something?" Emma said.

"If there isn't, I'm pretty sure it's at least part of the social contract. She's got like a Mason-Dixon line of shit going out there."

She snorted. "Yeah, if Trump's serious about that wall, he should just fly all the dogs to the border. Nobody would want to cross that. And, hey, if they're all Chihuahuas, wouldn't that be like they were paying for it?"

I flipped open my laptop and searched 'animal waste.'

"Apparently if it's in her yard we can't really do anything about it."

"I'm pretty sure that's technically our property."

"I guess I could try to say something to her but I don't think it would help. If she weren't doing it to be combative, it wouldn't be there in the first place."

"We could at least call and report it to animal control or something."

"I guess. But, I mean, it's going to be obvious who called. We're the only other people back here."

Emma let it drop. I was glad. We tried to shut the bad neighbor out of our thoughts. Or, rather, we just worked around her. We left the front blinds and the blinds on the neighbor's side closed at all times. We heard the dogs barking late at night and turned the music or the TV up or just laid our books in our laps, closed our eyes, and took deep breaths. We had moved out of the city because we were ready for some peace and quiet. We were ready to move forward with our lives. The neighbor was little more than a stumbling block. Broagies was an expanding franchise and increasingly popular. I was busier than ever. Emma had received a small pay bump from the Point and had to take on a few more responsibilities. We didn't need the hassle and anxiety that an all-out war with a neighbor would bring.

We busied ourselves with putting the finishing touches on the house and hoping our neighbor would meet some natural death.

FOUR

Of course the back door was locked.

We stood on the deck, a much shabbier version of our own. It didn't even feel safe to stand on and I imagined it creaking and bowing under Meg Chinaski's girth.

We backed up from the door, staring at our smudged reflections in the smeared and streaked glass.

"Are you sure you want to go through with this?" I asked. All the blood had rushed to my head. My heartbeat sounded thunderous in my ears.

Emma was smiling, the machete gripped firmly in her hand.

"I don't think I've ever wanted anything more."

When Emma came in the front door, one foot raised above the throw rug, I knew some action would have to be taken.

"I stepped in it again," she said. "You have to say something to that bitch."

"I will," I said. And I meant it. I hated conflict but I hated the hurt look on Emma's face even more. I hated the feeling of having worked hard for something only to have your spirit crushed when you finally achieved that thing.

"Okay," she said. "Then go do it." She took off the other shoe and went into the kitchen where she put both shoes in a plastic bag and tied it off.

"I'm not going to do it now."

"Why not?"

"What? I go over there and pound on her door? You think she's even going to open it if she sees it's me? She'll probably think I'm there to rape her. She'll probably come to the door with a shotgun."

Emma was angrily scrawling something onto a piece of paper.

"What are you doing?" I asked.

"Leaving that cunt a note."

I looked at what she'd written:

PLEASE WASH AND RETURN.
THANKS,
YOUR NEIGHBORS

She then stormed outside in her socks, marched to the edge of our driveway, and flung the bag so it landed perfectly on the neighbor's front stoop.

I thought it was a pretty badass thing to do but knew it probably wouldn't end well.

When we left for work the next morning, the bag lay in our front yard, returned with an equal fit of anger. No note was attached because we assumed the neighbor probably couldn't read or write. Emma marched the bag to the trashcan and dropped it in.

She got in the passenger side and said, "If she comes out with those dogs, you should just run the little shit machines over."

Sure enough, just as I backed out of the driveway and into the street, the neighbor's door opened, her immense frame filling the doorway.

Emma glared at her.

"Big bad bubba," she said. "Fucking hillbilly trash."

"She's just, like, a fucking bully," I said. "A hillbully."

I spoke to the neighbor for the first time shortly after that. Emma had picked me up from Broagies and we'd gone home. Pulling into the driveway, the neighbor was out with all three dogs.

"I know," I said before Emma could say anything. "I'll talk to her."

I got out of the passenger side and almost slammed the door on Emma, who was also getting out on the passenger side so she didn't have to deal with the shit and the barking and the hostile glares.

I told myself to be calm. Take some deep breaths. I'm not an argumentative or combative person but, in the few times I've been forced to, I usually just end up getting mean and basically making fun of who I'm arguing with. It's fairly childish and always leaves me feeling bad about myself, but it's the only thing I know to do. I had to tell myself that, at the heart of it, this was a woman—probably around the same age as my mother—and, being a man, I probably shouldn't physically threaten her or devolve into calling her things like 'bitch' or 'cunt' or 'white trash piece of shit' or anything like that.

I took another deep breath and thought, "Be civil."

I walked over to the edge of the driveway, staring down at the piles of shit lined up.

The dogs were less than a foot away from me, gnashing their teeth and straining against their leashes.

"Got a problem?" the neighbor asked.

And she must have felt a huge sense of satisfaction. Here was the confrontation she'd been begging for for the past two months. That's what she'd been hoping for. Every act had been one of aggression, a taunt, thirsty for retaliation. When the dogs were outside our window at night, she wanted one of us to stagger out in a half-drunk or half-asleep rage fugue and ask her what the fuck she thought she was doing. Just like Emma had said when we first moved in. I'd always just wanted to be left alone so this was behavior I didn't understand.

"Kind of," I said. "Do you think it's possible to keep your dogs away from the driveway a little bit? Maybe give us some space to at least get out of our car?"

"That ain't mine. You seen where I take my dogs. Up there by my house."

"I see you taking them all over. It's even down there by the street."

"Well, you shouldn'ta moved here if you don't like dogs. You knowed they was dogs in this neighborhood. Strays go all over. I know you've seen em."

In truth, we hadn't because we'd kept the house pretty much closed up because of this upright whale.

"This isn't from strays. And I definitely don't hate dogs but you shouldn't use them as weapons."

"Yer just mad cause you got suckered into buyin this place. Thought you got yerself a deal but it's covered in mold just like them other two no one's livin in. They's dead from mold. You'll feel like you got a deal when you's both in the hospital with lung infections. All they did was paint over it but it's in the walls . . . everywhere."

I was so baffled by the change of direction I was momentarily lost for words.

"I'm not trying to be a dick or anything just . . . give us some space, okay?"

The dogs had not stopped barking during this entire exchange and it finally dawned on me that I was accomplishing exactly nothing by trying to talk to this psychotic idiot. And the dog noise was so loud and constant I couldn't even manage to put together an argument that was as equally insane as the one she was giving me.

"You are," she said. "Think yer too good for this place. Throwin yer junk over into my yard. Wantin me to do yer laundry. Well I'm just waitin til you's both all packed up with mold."

She was even crazier than I'd thought so I started backing away. I tried to give her a smile.

"Anyway," I said, now shouting over the dogs, "I'm Kip! My wife's name is Emma! It was *great* meeting you, neighbor! You seem like a wonderful person!"

Then I turned to the house, listening to her tell her dogs what a fucking asshole I was.

I shut the door behind me and said, "That didn't go well."

That night we did our research.

Emma started by typing in the neighbor's address in a county records database.

"Meg Chinaski," she said. "House isn't paid off. Looks like she has a second mortgage on it."

"Chinaski," I said. "That sounds familiar."

I tapped on the wi-fi icon. There it was: 'Chinaski'. That must have been her handle. I promptly changed ours to 'SatanLovesChinaski' from whatever generic one we'd used since buying the router and felt a glimmer of satisfaction.

Then Emma typed her name into Google. We were thinking she was so crazy it would have to turn up some incident report or criminal record. Instead, the only thing it turned up was an obituary for her late husband, Gerald.

Emma shivered. "Oh, man, this means somebody actually fucked that bitch."

The obituary contained other information. He was 69 at his death, so we assumed she was probably around the same age. He was survived by his wife, Meg, and two children—Michelle and Kenneth—and one grandchild, no name given.

"If she has kids and a grandkid," Emma said, "she really must be a raging cunt if they don't come to visit her."

"Maybe they don't live around here or something."

Emma typed their names into Google.

"Well," she said, "it looks like the son's in jail and the daughter lives pretty close. She looks like a party girl."

Emma smirked and turned her laptop to face me. She clicked through the images, revealing a beefy, overly tanned, bleached blond woman who looked around forty—a really hard forty—and wore clothes a lot more tight-fitting than she should probably wear.

"Yikes," I said.

We didn't turn up anything else significant and I didn't know what we were supposed to do with the information we'd obtained. I guess it was knowledge and they say knowledge equals power.

Emma went to the city's website and reported her for all the dog shit in the yard. I thought it was unlikely they'd do anything about it.

"One thing's for sure," I said. "I'm not trying to talk to her again."

I held that promise until one evening over the winter when I took the trashcans down to the curb. Chinaski was, of course, out there with her dogs. They started yapping and lurching as soon as they noticed me. I tried to tune it out. Told myself she probably wouldn't say anything to me. Probably just wanted to be left alone. And I couldn't just lay into her out of the blue, even though there were about a million things I wanted to say to her, not that any of them would have done any good.

I heard her mumble something and glanced in her direction, thinking she was probably talking to the dogs, even though what she was saying was probably about me.

She was looking directly at me.

"Sorry?" I said.

There was still a part of me that wanted to think all of our suppositions about her were completely in our own heads. Maybe she wasn't an antagonistic, malicious, combative hillbully. Part of me wanted to think she'd possibly uttered something neighborly:

"Gonna be gettin cold soon." Or "How you likin the new place?"

What she said, apparently, from what I could hear through the swirl of barking dogs, was: "You think you could make any more noise?"

Once again, she'd taken me completely off-guard.

"I was, uh, just bringing the trash down." But I should have just walked away. She wanted to rant and vent. She wanted nothing resembling a rational discussion.

"Every night!" she squawked. "Every night yer up all night. Sleepin all day. Yer a motherfuckin alcoholic!"

At this point, I was again stumped. Emma and I did stay up late on the weekends watching movies and, sometimes, we had a few drinks, but it wasn't like we were having a party in there or anything. And it wasn't like it was any of Chinaski's business if we were. It was only just the two of us. And, unlike our neighbor, we actually woke up and left the house by nine to go to work. True, we didn't typically get out of bed before noon on the weekends but that was because we were fucking adults and didn't have to.

I knew there was no arguing with her so I began walking back to the house.

Then I thought, what the fuck? She's already riled up.

So I doubled back.

"What's your problem with us?" I shouted over the dogs.

"I done told you. You's a fuckin alcoholic drunky. In there all night carryin on with yer drinkin and witchcraft!"

The witchcraft was a new one and threatened to again derail me.

"Hey," I said, "I think we're decent neighbors. If we do something that bothers you, let us know."

"S'what I'm doin, motherfucker!"

Now she was walking toward me, the dogs leaping against their leashes, barking furiously, and she was muttering, "Get him. Get him," to the dogs even though she never let go of the leashes.

I dismissively waved my hands at her, figuratively throwing the whole situation into the trash, before going back inside to relay the whole scenario to Emma.

"So," Emma said, "let's see. We're alcoholics because we stay up too late a couple nights a week. But she wouldn't know we were up that late if she wasn't standing in her front yard staring at our house like a bloated fucking creep. Oh, and she probably sits in there and listens for the sound of us taking out the recycling. I'm pretty sure she mumbled 'Bar's closed' last time I did that. I wanted to turn to her and say, 'Bitch, it's only two in the afternoon, bar's just now opening!'

"Noise? Again, there's no way she can hear us from inside her house.

Not over that fucking air conditioner that runs non-stop. So again, the only reason she ever hears us make a sound is because she's standing outside ten feet from our fucking living room window."

"What about the witchcraft?"

"Fuck. I don't know. I have tattoos. We drive a black car. We both wear a lot of black. We listen to evil music. Well, when we're not listening to NPR. That's probably the most evil thing in the world to people like her. Wait, no, people like her are too stupid to even know what NPR is."

"Okay . . ." I said. "So she's basically just batshit fucking crazy."

"She's the problem. We're not the problem."

FIVE

The night would have seemed quiet if we were not now less than five feet from the roaring, sputtering air conditioner. It faded the line between what should have been a quiet, residential cul-de-sac on a mid-summer evening and the inevitable chaos of what we would find inside Chinaski's house.

"On the count of three," Emma said, hoisting her brick up to shoulder-level and cocking her arm.

I did the same.

"One," Emma breathed.

My insides felt drawn tight, my arm shaking. I hoped I'd be able to find the strength to throw the brick hard enough to break the window.

"Two."

Probably the best thing that could happen was for something to go terribly wrong. For the bricks to not go through the glass. For the glass to shatter only for us to realize Chinaski wasn't too poor for an alarm system. For a light to click on at that exact moment, her ghoulish face filling the window as she peered out to see the potential, easily identifiable intruders.

If I was going to say something, it had to be now.

"Three."

Too late.

Emma's brick shattered the glass. Mine hit far down on the metal frame in between the two doors.

The dogs were immediately alert, yapping and padding toward the door.

I heard Chinaski cough from somewhere in the house.

I was at Broagies on a Sunday. Even though I was the manager, I usually took Sundays off. I was there mainly to train Shawn Bibbles. I preferred to do all the training so new employees wouldn't learn any bad habits right out of the gate and Sunday was the only day Shawn was available to come in. We were pretty short-handed and I needed to get him up to speed as soon as possible.

"It's pretty simple," I said, standing behind the counter, Shawn next to me. "You start with the butcher paper." I reached up to the roll and tugged down a sheet of perforated paper. I pointed to an arrow on the left side of the perforations. "They want small, you stop and tear it at the first arrow. They want a medium, you do the second arrow. Large, the third. Pretty easy, huh?"

Shawn didn't answer.

I glanced at him and noticed he'd slid his phone from the pocket of his pants and was tapping something into it.

"You paying attention, Shawn?"

"I'm trying, man. It's real hard for me to focus."

"That's okay. It'll get easier." I tried not to criticize any of my employees, especially the younger ones. They seemed to get their feelings hurt pretty easily. Take, for instance, the fact that Shawn had arrived in sweat pants. I immediately thought about telling him he couldn't come to work in sweat pants before deciding it was ultimately my fault. Or at least the fault of the Broagies franchise literature. It stated that pants must be black. It didn't specifically state they couldn't be sweat pants. I knew for sure because I went back and read it about five times while Shawn alternated between filling out his paperwork and checking his phone.

I watched him as he typed the last of something in his phone and dropped it into his pocket.

"Texting a bud or are you on MyFace?" I liked trying to connect with my younger employees.

"I don't remember, man." Shawn dazedly blinked.

"I met my wife on MyFace."

"Nobody really uses that anymore."

I felt old, like I'd said we'd met at a flapper dance or an ice cream cordial.

"Yeah. Cool, man. I haven't used it in a while myself. So, okay, back to the broagie . . . We have three bread choices . . . Have you ever eaten at a Broagies before?"

Shawn shrugged and I didn't really know what that meant.

"Okay, so there are three bread choices: white, wheat, and gluten free. If they order gluten free, you're supposed to offer them a second fist bump. This is so they don't feel so weird and alienated with their choice. You want to make them think they made the right decision but they've really just been upsold because we charge an extra two dollars for the gluten free. Do you need to tell them there's an extra charge though? Absolutely not because it's right there on the menu board."

I turned to gesture at the menu board. Shawn turned slowly to do the same thing, but raising his head to actually look at the board must have thrown off his equilibrium or something because he stumbled back and collapsed onto the floor.

"You okay, man?" I asked.

He smiled a little and shook his head. "I think so. That was a tough move."

I extended my hand to help him up, grateful there wasn't anyone else in the store.

He didn't take my hand, opting to try it himself. He tried to push himself up but tumbled back onto his doughy ass and laughed. "This is really hard!" he said.

"You can do it, man."

He managed to get to his knees and grab the edge of the counter with his fingertips before proceeding to pull himself up from the floor with all the effort of someone escaping a whirlpool.

By the time he made it to his feet, he was breathing heavily.

I clapped him on the back.

"Shake it off, bro."

I gave him a few seconds before asking, "Are you good?"

"I don't know," he said.

"Okay, so then you ask them how hard they want to bro today. Some guests will not know what that means and you can just ask them what they want on their broagie."

Shawn's back was to me, his phone in his hands.

I watched him type a message that said: "I gist fel don!"

"Shawn?"

"Oh." He seemed surprised I was talking. "I forgot what I was doing."

"It's okay, man. Let me know if you're not getting anything and we can start over."

He stared at my chest and squinted.

"What's happening, like, right now?" he said.

"Let's go back to the beginning," I said.

I walked him back to the butcher paper. His phone never went back into his pocket. There were sounds coming from it and I assumed he was watching a MeTube video or possibly even pornography.

"This is the butcher paper," I said. "This is where we start."

Shawn wandered out from behind the counter and sat at a table.

My phone vibrated in my pocket. I pulled it out. It was Emma. She never called me at work.

I answered it.

"What's up?" I said.

"Can you come home?"

"Um, I'm training a new guy. I guess I can see if Chloe can come in."

"Would you?"

"What's up?"

"The neighbor. She's been standing on the sidewalk and staring at our house all day. I wanted to weed the flowerbeds. She brings one dog out and then goes back in and then I come out and she brings another dog out. Then she starts murmuring about witches getting burned and says at least she knows who's been breaking into her car at night. She's standing out there now with a pair of lawn shears. I'm . . . kind of afraid."

"Okay. Well, lock the doors. I'll be there as soon as I can. If you feel threatened, you should call the police. We probably need to start keeping a record of the crazy shit she does."

"I know. I'm probably overreacting."

I hung up with Emma and called Chloe, who said she could come in in about a half an hour.

I went back to the counter to find Shawn standing on the other side.

"Can I order a broagie, dude?" he asked.

"Sure, man, whaddya want?"

"What is a broagie? Is it like a sandwich or something?"

"Yeah, man, it's like a hoagie. Only vegan."

"I just want chips then. You guys got chips?"

I pointed to the rack.

"Whatever's fine, man."

He was still trying to figure out how to pay by the time Chloe got there. He just kept tapping different apps, as though one of them would vomit money like a slot machine.

When I got home, the neighbor was no longer standing outside. Part of me hoped Emma had called the police.

But she hadn't.

Lying in bed that night, she told me why.

SIX

There was an immediate explosion of chaos and I panicked.

I kicked the first dog so hard, just to get it away from me, that it flew across the room and hit the far wall, bouncing onto the floor in a twitching, broken heap.

Chinaski's house was exactly the same as ours and Emma turned toward the bedroom with her machete at the ready.

I reached down and snatched the second dog up by the collar. The third one was old and fat and wasn't barking. Didn't really seem to know what was going on at all. I started to cross the darkened living room when a movement to my right caught my attention.

Chinaski stood in the small foyer created between the doors of the two bedrooms and the bathroom. She stood looking into the second bedroom, the one where Emma had gone.

Fuck.

We'd gotten it wrong.

Chinaski had an old looking rifle. Her girth gave it the scale of a toy gun.

I lost it.

I couldn't imagine anything happening to Emma and, luckily, hadn't really had to up to this point.

With the dog still kicking and yapping in my left hand, I held the knife in front of me and charged at the massive hillbully. Already closer than I'd ever physically been to her, I watched her get bigger and bigger.

I aimed for the back of her neck and the knife plunged into her easily.

The gun blast was deafening in the small house.

I heard Emma cry out.

I slid the knife out and plunged it in several more times along her back.

Why did I think this would be hard?

Eventually she collapsed forward, leaving me covered in the iron stink of her blood and the gamey scent of her presence.

"Why didn't you just call the cops?" I asked.

Emma was silent, her hands resting on her tiny breasts.

"Were you afraid?"

"I was afraid of her. I wasn't afraid of calling the cops. I just . . . didn't want to."

"Why not?"

She chuffed out a cough and said, "Do you really think they're going to do anything about something minor like that?"

"I don't know. It seems like the dog shit is definitely breaking a law. And the staring and dog barking and insults have to be like harassment or menacing or something. Right?"

"Probably."

"So why not?"

"There may come a day when the most efficient way to handle this . . . problem is to take care of it ourselves." There was a tone in her voice I'd never really heard before. The potential for it had probably, realistically, always been there. It was probably one of the reasons I'd fallen in love with her.

"And if it comes to that," she continued, "it wouldn't look at all good if there's a list of complaints lodged by us sitting on the police's hard drive."

I lay there in silence, rendered completely speechless. We were in the darkened, quiet bedroom of our first home, the only light coming from a flickering late night talk show on the small television. It seemed like the most banal scene ever but what Emma seemed to be proposing was complete and total insanity.

"That's . . . that's kinda nuts, Em."

"Is it? I'll tell you what's crazy. This is our dream, Kip. It's not perfect, sure, but it's the start of everything we've worked our entire lives for. And since the day we've moved in here she has been literally shitting on that dream. Not figuratively. Not metaphorically. Literally. Yet we're the ones who are not doing anything wrong. Still, we're supposed to bend our lives to the will of her insanity. I know you don't like conflict and arguments. I don't like them either. You know that. But I'm not going to sit back and watch that bitch piss and shit all over us. I'm not going to waste a second of our time trying to reason with her, or get the cops to reason with her, or get her the kind of help she undoubtedly needs. I'm not going to do that because I shouldn't have to. You can tell yourself she's going to change. You can tell yourself we just got off on the wrong foot and if we're nice to her eventually she'll come around. But I'm telling you that's not going to happen. There's some dark force surrounding her and she's trying to pull us into it. She just sits over there all day with those stupid fucking little shit bombs and focuses on ways to make our lives miserable. She doesn't go anywhere. Nobody ever comes to see her. We're all she has. And she's not going to go away unless *we* do something about her."

I smiled and laughed a little. "A dark force?"

"It's not funny."

"Come on. It's kind of funny."

That conversation happened in the fall of last year.

As with most things, I just tried to forget about it and hope it would go away. After all, it was getting cooler outside and Chinaski hadn't been outside that much last winter and, while her bizarre behavior had ramped up considerably over the summer, I was hoping a new year would bring about a change.

But it didn't.

She started ranting at night as we sat in the living room. Always in the form of dialogue with her dogs and at a volume low enough to prevent us from hearing the exact words. Some nights she stood out there whistling and some nights she laughed like a lunatic. It was always with the dogs, who were usually yapping away the entire time, further obscuring whatever she may have been saying or doing. Never for more than five or ten minutes at a time. When we left for work, she was out there. When we got home, she was there. She waited for us to take out the trash, standing blank-eyed, her mongrels' leashes clutched in her beefy hand. We planned retorts and comebacks but, most times, she didn't say anything to us, almost to the point of us asking ourselves if she'd *ever* said anything to us. And then we'd let our guard down and she'd accuse us of making bombs in the basement or operating what she called a 'kiddie fuck ring.' It was always so bizarre I couldn't do anything but tilt my head and stare quizzically at the stained crazy woman standing in a foot of snow.

Over the winter, Emma began researching spells and magick online. Maybe she tried some of the stuff. I don't know. I was never a believer. And if she did, none of it worked.

We talked about gaslighting Chinaski but I pointed out that would probably only work if she were sane to start with.

Fortunately it was winter so we had an excuse to not go outside, didn't feel like we were missing out on anything by not doing it. Chinaski continued to wage her war, however. We'd glance out through the blinds to see her vacantly walking one or more of her dogs around the yard. While she didn't shovel her driveway or sidewalk, she did shovel off a small section of the lawn—something I'd never really seen anyone do before—and this was where she walked her dogs. Then, of course, we'd hear her all night, she hacking and muttering, the dogs yapping and yapping.

Then, for a period of about two weeks, she seemed to disappear.

We didn't hear her.

We didn't see her.

It was a glorious respite.

"I haven't seen or heard her in, like, two weeks," Emma said over dinner one night.

I hadn't mentioned it. I was a little superstitious about things like that. Like teammates not saying anything when their pitcher is throwing a no-hitter.

"Maybe she died," I said.

"It would be too good to be true."

Given her age and body type, it wasn't an unrealistic expectation. People get that big, especially if they don't take care of themselves at all, and their heart just gives out. Plus she probably never went to the doctor. There could be a lot of undiagnosed cancer running around in that massive playground. Unless she ran on evil, I thought. It seemed like people who ran on hate and evil had the ability to live forever.

"Maybe she slipped and fell," I said.

We'd often entertained thoughts of coming home to find her frozen, Jack Torrance-style, in her front yard. We both agreed we wouldn't offer to help and would wait at least twenty-four hours before calling anyone. We didn't know if that would be criminal or not and, quite honestly, didn't care.

Late that night, as if just referencing it invoked some psychic darkness, we heard her.

"Fuck," Emma muttered. She'd been lying on the couch browsing through a brochure for spring bulbs to plant in the front yard once the weather broke. She threw the brochure across the room.

I, too, had been lost in a reverie of hope and dread. The hopeful part of me envisioned a spring and summer of hard work and recreation. The yard and the outside of the house still needed cleaning up. I was raised on a farm and loved being outside, loved breaking a sweat while enjoying the sights and sounds and smells of nature. While there had been a decent park area near our downtown apartment, it felt contrived and manmade and was, let's face it, basically just an outdoor hotel for the homeless. Hardly relaxing. Other than the rare hiking excursion to Twin Springs, that nature-longing part of me had been sorely met. I wanted days of being out in the sun and nights of unwinding on the deck with a beer and the company of Emma.

The dread stemmed from the thought of who would move in after her if she had died. I figured it could go either way but, in the end, the dread was softened because I didn't really see how it could be much worse unless it were like a family of hillbillies who actually shot at the house or something. I'd lived a lot of places my entire life, had many neighbors, and hadn't had a problem with a single one of them.

But that was all wiped clean with the cacophony of barking dogs and I was back to that place of feeling trapped, of feeling like I'd made a terrible mistake, of feeling like I'd contributed to the purchase of a prison, not a home for my wife and I.

I Googled 'how to get out of a mortgage.'

Emma said, "So if she can not come out of her house for two weeks at a time, it means she really does bring them out there just to torture us."

Emma brought up a good point. What did she do with them when she didn't bring them outside? I imagined Chinaski sitting around in her moldy little house, surrounded by little piles of dog shit. Or maybe she didn't want to deal with it. Maybe she just locked them in the basement and let them go down there. After all, she'd probably be dead before it became too big a problem. Let someone else deal with it after she was gone. Or maybe she just caught them when they were ready to go, held them up over her head, and let them shit in her mouth, eliciting a response almost sexual in nature. I imagined what her life must be like. All time and attention spent on those dogs. There was clearly no love in the woman's heart. I'd never heard her utter a single kind word to any of the dogs—so the drive for someone so obviously lazy and hateful almost had to be sexual. That is, she wasn't into the zen-like ritual of maintaining them. Her days were filled with dragging them inside and out, standing out there in the yard, focusing in on their little dog assholes, waiting for them to dilate and those brown ropes of shit to slide out. I imagined her getting inside and taking off her shoes, noticing she'd stepped in a pile she couldn't see over her enormous torso, bringing the shoe up to her nose and breathing in the aroma as though sampling the bouquet of a fine wine, a slight moistening between her legs as the love of dog shit massaged whatever dim pleasure center rotted away in her fat head.

The first warm week drew to a close and Emma mentioned taking care of our problem for the first time since that winter. It was a week of perfect weather. The time had changed so we had an extra hour of daylight and we divided our time between work and staying inside with the windows shut and the blinds drawn. Normally, even living downtown, it would have been that much heralded first week when you can lie in bed with the windows open, listening to the sound of the world warming up and coming back to life.

Instead, we lay in bed with the house fan running to keep it from feeling too stuffy.

"This is ridiculous," Emma said.

"There has to be something we can do about it," I said.

"There is."

"Not that."

"I'm starting to think it's the only way. She's not really doing anything illegal. You can't call the cops on people for being annoying. And even if you could, it's not going to make her go away. She *needs* to go away."

"I know."

"I don't want to spend another summer locked up in the house. Look at us. We've both taken on so much responsibility at our jobs, sometimes working fifty-plus hours a week because neither one of us wants to come home anymore. We have hundreds of dollars' worth of deck furniture we haven't even bothered dragging out of the garage since we bought it. We bought a grill that's been used exactly once. We should have been out all weekend planting flowers and playing outside and instead we stayed inside and binge-watched nearly every season of *Dan Banal*. And we'd seen them all before. And it's not even very good!"

I could sense Emma getting worked up.

I said, "Have you thought about putting the house up for sale? We'll be at the two-year mark toward the end of summer so we won't have to pay the inflated earnings tax."

"No. If we move, it means she wins."

"Maybe it's more than just her. Maybe we made a mistake. Maybe this area just isn't for us. Maybe we should just move back downtown."

"We can't afford to. Plus we overpaid for this place. We probably wouldn't even get what we owe for it."

"So . . . what? We kill her?"

Emma smiled. "You're the one who said it."

"Hey, wait. I wasn't—"

"Think about it, Kip. We're both bright people. We can figure out how to cover our tracks. Neither one of us has a criminal record. There's no one back here. It's not like we would ever be caught in the act. It would probably be weeks before anyone even noticed. And who's to notice, anyway? Maybe the mailman says something after her mailbox fills up and he notices an odd smell coming from the house. But maybe he doesn't say anything either. You've seen the way she terrorizes him with her dogs. So maybe he still delivers the mail until the mailbox is too full and puts a hold on her account. Maybe she just disappears. Who's to know? Who's to care? It happens all the time. People would just assume she couldn't keep up on her bills or house payment and just moved in with one of her kids or something. No one's going to try tracking her down. Think about it. We put her on trial when we moved in here. A trial with a two-person jury. We're open-minded, forgiving people. We have given her every chance to prove her innocence—even simply her compliance to the social contract—and she just keeps getting more and more insufferable. It's like tribal law and that law has found her guilty."

"Okay," I said, more or less to get her to stop talking about it.

We spent the next month hammering out the details.

SEVEN

And I'd fucked it up.

I was supposed to handle the dogs and Emma was to take care of Chinaski.

Now I stood over Chinaski's well-stabbed corpse, one of her dogs writhing and yapping and gurgling in my left hand, the other remaining one sniffing obliviously around my ankles.

The only thing I could think about was Emma.

"Emma!" I called.

Between the gun blast and the barking dog, I was having trouble hearing much of anything else.

The dog was making me furious.

I held it out in front of me and stabbed at it until it was quiet and then flung it back over my shoulder.

"Emma!" I called again.

She emerged from the bedroom, her fingers plunged into her ears. She jostled them like she was trying to get some water out.

She seemed to be moving okay.

I didn't see any blood on her but she was wearing all black so it was impossible to tell.

"Are you okay?" I asked.

She now stood over Chinaski's corpse.

"Oh, Kip," she said.

"Emma?"

She moved closer to me and placed her head against my chest.

"Oh, Kip." She raised her face to mine. She was beaming a radiant smile. "I've never been better."

I dropped the knife and took her in my arms, rubbing my hands over her black-clad curves, possibly to make sure I didn't feel any blood. I was still shaking with adrenaline and, the more I explored her, the more I convinced myself she truly was unharmed, the more I felt like crying.

She pulled away a little and made a pouty face.

"What's wrong, Em?"

She looked down at Chinaski's bloated corpse.

"You knew I wanted to do it."

And then I did break down. Because what she said was so banal. So petty. So Emma.

She wiped a tear from my cheek and said, "Oh, Kip, I know you did what you had to."

"You know," I said, "she's still right there."

Then Emma pulled me down to her and I felt her hot breath in my ear saying, "I love you so much."

The old fat dog was now sniffing around Chinaski's corpse, lapping at the blood.

I felt Emma's hand brush my cock and was surprised to note that I was hard.

Then my lips were on Emma's and after that everything became something of a blur. Clothes were removed and tossed wherever. Emma was in my hands and I was in hers. We attacked each other like it was our first month together, ascending to such a plane that I felt close to blacking out.

I recall Emma stabbing Chinaski's corpse repeatedly, dipping her hands in the offal and rubbing it all over her beautiful pale body, shouting, "I never thought bathing in someone else's blood would feel so good!"

And she was right.

We didn't leave Chinaski's house until just before dawn.

We spared the final dog, letting it wander out into the yard before exiting out the way we'd come.

Still, outside, the sound of the infernal air conditioner. It would be months before she got so behind on her electric bill they shut it off.

I pulled the bloody machete out of Emma's hand and rammed it through the grate at the top of the unit. Just stopping the fan already reduced the noise. I felt like it would only be a matter of time before it overheated and blew up.

Exhausted, we went back to our house.

Emma collapsed onto the bed wearing only her bra and panties, covered in blood and who knew how many of our own bodily fluids. I wore just my underwear, black to begin with but now sodden with the same substances.

I turned to Emma and smiled.

I opened up our bedroom windows and collapsed next to her.

We heard a high-pitched whine shriek from the air conditioner and then the only sound in the room was the soft hum of the cicadas and a few early birds. Emma moved into me. I put my arm around her and she put hers over my chest.

I thought I would feel bad.

I thought I would feel guilty.

But I didn't.

I felt relieved.

EIGHT

We woke up the next afternoon to a sound we hadn't heard since moving here: children playing.

There would have been a time when I would have found this annoying but, after the past two years, it was nearly soothing.

I turned my head to look at Emma, awake and smiling behind her mask of dried blood.

"I know," she said. "I think I even hear an ice cream truck."

I had to see what was going on. I threw on a thin robe and staggered toward the front door.

I pulled it open, greeted by the sunlight.

A couple of kids—a boy and a girl—rode their bicycles around the cul-de-sac. I glanced at one of the houses on the ends and saw what may have been their parents, emerging from the house like liberated concentration camp survivors. They threw their heads up at the blue sky and, even from this distance, I could see the smiles on their faces.

I raised my hand in a wave.

They did the same.

I was startled by a couple walking up the sidewalk from the right.

They also looked pale and emaciated yet, strangely, full of life and energy.

The woman jerked her head toward Chinaski's house and said, "We were thinkin bonfire."

I laughed and said, "We'll bring the hot dogs!"

Introductions were made all the way around. They didn't seem too concerned about the blood. Maybe they just saw it as a common sign of living in a war zone.

I closed the door and walked back into the house, feeling as hopeful as I had the first day we'd moved in.

"We did the right thing," I said to Emma.

Now maybe we could begin the life we had been trying to live.

That night we sat on the deck with beers, watching the lightning bugs chase each other around the backyard and listening to the katydids and cicadas punctuate the sleepy hum of the distant highway.

The old fat dog came around the corner of the house, its teeth clamped around a purple diabetic ankle.

"Cheers," I said.

Emma and I clicked our bottles in a toast.

WE

DON'T

TALK

ABOUT

HER

ONE

"Your lover's back," Jaime said.

Stella had her back turned to the counter, dumping some flavoring in a housewife's double caramel macchiato with extra whipped cream.

"Ugh," Stella said, knowing immediately who Jaime was talking about, the guy Stella lovingly referred to as "Mr. Stalky."

"What the hell is he wearing?"

Mr. Stalky was so named not only because of his overall creepy demeanor but because they had no idea what his real name was. As far as she knew, he'd only ever paid cash for anything and had always refused to sign up for their loyalty rewards program, even though he was there at least a couple times a week. That wasn't to say she knew *nothing* about him. The things you could find out about a person by the way they dressed or acted said way more about who they were than their name. Not to mention what one could find out if she did only the slightest bit of reconnaissance. He always ordered a small cup of black coffee "with plenty room for ice." Always came in around nine p.m. and stayed until they told him they'd be closing an hour later. He was usually the last one there.

Just another Friday at Jungle Books. It was technically a bookstore but they didn't really carry that many books. The owner was, she guessed, a Kipling fan, and the place was decorated with a lot of exotic plants and dark wood shelves and tables and chairs, the ceiling fans with the blades shaped like broad palm fronds. Most people came there for the coffee and tea. Most people got it to go. The ones who stuck around, she assumed, were either recovering alcoholics who couldn't go to a bar to sit and drink anymore or people too young to go to a bar. The ones who weren't in groups just sat around looking at their phones with either hollow-eyed stares or warm, nearly ecstatic glows. Kind of made it feel like being in a bar. But, like, a really sad bar.

She'd never seen Mr. Stalky looking at a book or a phone. Tonight he was wandering around looking at some of the vintage paintings depicting the more romantic elements of colonialism while quickly glancing over his shoulder so he could time his arrival to the counter with Stella's ability to help him. And, yes, Jaime was right. Stella had no idea what he was wearing. There was the relatively generic but heavily stained polo shirt he seemed to always wear but his usual weird dad jeans were replaced with, she didn't know, something . . . wrapped. Not bandages. Either paper towels or toilet paper, if she had to guess. Like he was going to a costume party as the mummy, even though it was nowhere near Halloween.

Stella put the lid on the macchiato and slid it across the counter.

Jaime called across the store to Mr. Stalky, "I can help you, sir."

He turned and approached the counter.

By the time he got there, the woman before him was already walking away.

Even though Jaime was in position behind her register, Mr. Stalky stepped directly in front of Stella and ordered his small coffee with plenty room for ice. Not an iced coffee. He just thought they served it too hot.

"The usual, huh?" Stella said.

"You bet," he said. "That's about the only thing usual for today though, for sure."

He tried to do this a lot. It wasn't an uncommon ploy for desperate people his age, which she put somewhere in his late thirties or forties. It wasn't just men. A lot of lonely women would throw out these vague kinds of statements to try and engage the baristas in conversation. Stella wasn't really much of a conversationalist—this was just a job, after all, plus she found most people to be hopelessly mundane or just extremely boring—so she rarely let herself get roped in by their attempted engagements. Besides, she liked to find out about people herself, rather than assuming anything they said about themselves was remotely true. Everyone edited their lives. If she were to know anything, she wanted the rough draft.

"I mean," he said, "I'm sure you've noticed my pants."

Stella turned to pour his coffee and dropped in a few ice cubes. She didn't put the lid on because she knew he would just take it over to the milk bar and dump about six packs of sugar into it.

She tried her best to smile and said, "Now what's so unusual about your pants?"

"I know you're gonna think this sounds crazy, Stella, but when I went to try and find my jeans this mornin, I couldn't find *a single pair*. Like somebody just broke in the house and stole em while I was sleepin."

"Hm," she said. "That is kind of unusual. Do you live with anybody else?"

"Just my ma and I don't see what she woulda done to my pants. She hardly moves anyway. I couldn't find em nowhere. Looked all over. So I had to make do."

"Hm," she said again. "Maybe you left them in the wash or something?" She bit her lip after asking this question. She was engaging him. Exactly what he wanted. The momentary loss of control was nearly debilitating.

"I doubt that," he said. "Pretty sure somebody stole em. Probably traded em in and now they's havin a fancy steak dinner. They was pretty nice pants. Slacks, really. Built-in belt and everything."

"Well that . . . certainly is something." She felt like she had gained at least some semblance of control. She wasn't going to ask any more questions.

"You're too nice." He slid across a few dollars that looked like they'd been dug from the ground and she gave him his exact change. He never tipped. She didn't know if he was stingy or just didn't understand the concept.

He took his coffee, added his sugar, put the lid on it, and sat down at one of the tables, facing the counter.

This was when he made Stella the most nervous. Well, not really nervous, because she wasn't afraid of him in the slightest. He could be dangerous, she had no doubt, but it didn't really matter to her. She could take care of herself. It was more the way he just sat there and glanced up from his coffee to let his gaze linger on the women behind the counter like they were the entertainment. Luckily, since it was nearly closing time, they had plenty of things to do, or at least pretend to do, and didn't have to stand around and awkwardly pretend they didn't notice him ogling them.

Stella bent down and slid a box of cups from under the counter. Jaime crouched down next to her.

"What was that story about his pants? I keep waiting for him to just bust out of those things."

"Is it paper towels or toilet paper?" Stella tried not to laugh.

"I don't know. Should we ask?"

"I don't think you really want to know."

Stella continued cleaning up behind the counter, getting it ready for the openers, while Jaime went out to the floor to straighten books that didn't need straightening and dust plants that didn't need dusting. When it got close to closing, Jaime took the honor of telling Mr. Stalky.

He stood and said, "I'll get outta yer hair then," tossed his mostly full cup in the trash, and headed out the front door.

His weird pants had indeed busted open, a rip down the back revealing a black cavern Stella assumed was the crack of his pudgy ass. She didn't want to imagine the unholiness contained therein.

"What a fucking weirdo," Jaime said.

TWO

Clint Mackey sat in his car, sipping his Venom energy drink and watching the two girls lock the front door of Jungle Books. He wished the cafe sold energy drinks. Especially an affordable one that made him feel like a lethal reptile. He always ordered coffee but he could barely choke the stuff down no matter how much sugar he added. It felt like such a waste. His Venom was sweet and fruity and fizzy and always made him feel good. Well, he supposed it did, anyway. He'd been drinking it for so long now he didn't really know what it would feel like to not have one of them in his system at all times.

Today had been a rough, stressful day. But watching the two girls now—especially Stella—made him feel relaxed and at ease. They each lit cigarettes and chatted inaudibly while they smoked them. He knew Jaime was in walking distance to her downtown apartment, but Stella had a car so she must live farther away. They were probably standing there smoking because they were the type of people who didn't smoke in their cars. Clint thought smoking was a pretty disgusting habit but he wouldn't care if Stella smoked in his car. It wouldn't really matter, filled up with trash like it was. He softly filled in words for the girls as they spoke.

Stella said, "I'm so lonely."

Jaime said, "Not me. I'm going home to my girlfriend because I'm a real hot lesbian."

Stella said, "You're so lucky. I'm so horny all the time and it's been a really long time since I've had sex. In fact, I'm a virgin. I just haven't found the right guy."

Jaime said, "You should ask that guy—Room For Ice—out. He's a little weird but I bet he's really nice. He'd treat you real good. Ha ha ha. Room For Ice is really nice! It rhymes, see? I can do that cause I'm so smart and funny and shit."

Stella said, "I couldn't stop looking at his cock in those pants."

Jaime said, "I'm sure he'd give it to you if you asked. I noticed it too."

Jaime placed a hand on Stella's forearm, the girls shared a laugh, and Clint felt like he had timed the dialogue perfectly. Probably because it was exactly what they were saying.

Before parting ways, Clint imagined Jaime saying, "I'm going to go home and shave my pussy!"

And he imagined Stella replying, "Not me. No need. I'm just going to whip up some popcorn and watch movies before masturbating to Mr. Dreamboat Room For Ice!"

Like that, he was so erect his penis burst through the two-ply toilet paper he'd taped around himself. Just the thought of it made him furious. He didn't want to go home. It seemed way too early. But it made him uncomfortable to drive around with his cock hanging out of his pants. He'd done it before but never without any way of putting it back.

Jaime walked toward the end of the street, bathed in lights. Stella went around the side of the building, into the alley parking lot where her car was parked. A few minutes later she pulled out and turned right.

Clint hesitated just a moment. He wasn't sure how much gas he had in the car and wasn't sure how far away she lived. He had a little bit of cash if he needed to buy more, but Ma's check wouldn't be coming for another two weeks and he needed to stretch what he had. Especially if he was going to have to buy new pants.

But he was still too mad at Ma and couldn't think of anything else to do.

Then he thought about standing by a gas pump with his dick hanging out.

He waited for Stella to stop at a red light far down the street before pulling his car away from the curb.

He hoped he didn't have to stop for gas.

THREE

"Well I'll just take it off and throw it in the humpin trash then!" Earlier that day, Clint had rolled off Ma and stormed around the overstuffed bedroom. His penis was coated in a foul-smelling slime. Despite giving it his best effort, Ma still just lay there, expressionless, not saying anything.

He wanted to storm around more, felt like he needed to, but not in this room. Here, it was just two steps and—*bam*—a wall of old greeting cards, two more steps the other way and—*bam*—a stack of about twenty-five disposable litter boxes, all used. He didn't want to knock those over again. Couldn't even remember the last time they'd had a cat.

"I can't even . . . You gotta clean this place up . . . I gotta get outta here!"

Clint stalked out of the room and didn't even look back at Ma. He felt like maybe she needed something. Some help of some kind but she'd been very adamant she didn't want nobody here, nobody going through their business, right up until she'd stopped talking some time back. He tried his best to keep her clean and whatnot, but she was really starting to smell bad even though she hadn't gone to the bathroom in forever. It made him sadder and sadder. He'd hoped she'd get to feeling better eventually if he just attended to her in the right way but she kept looking worse and worse.

The rest of the house was as packed with her stuff as the bedroom and he shuffled through pathways coated in old newspapers and fast food bags until he found the front door and threw it open and stepped out into the humid early evening heat. Once outside he took a deep breath and looked at the orange sun, mellowing on its way down to the horizon.

From right here on the front porch, there wasn't another house in sight and he felt good, that little shimmer of freedom like every time he managed to get out of the house, away from Ma.

He went over to the well and brought up a bucket of water and splashed some of it onto his junk until he thought it was about as clean as it was going to get without soap or a washcloth.

He sat on the front step and watched the sun slowly sink and thought maybe tonight would be a good night to go to Jungle Books. Back when Ma was more ambulatory, he was never allowed to go downtown. She'd hide his car keys from him unless he was going to the store for groceries. And she'd check the mileage too. She'd know if he went anywhere else. But now the car was all his since she couldn't even get out of bed. Sometimes he felt kind of bad for leaving her for a few hours but what did it really matter? She never moved. The more he thought about it, the more he preferred her this way. She hardly ever told him what to do anymore. Sometimes that just made things more frustrating because he didn't always know what he was *supposed* to do but it was still mostly all right. She didn't eat anything anymore, so he could use more of her check for energy drinks and snacks, which was all he really wanted. And now he had the freedom to go downtown every once in a while. Not that he really explored too much. Jungle Books was the only place he'd been. He'd driven downtown the first time and thought there would be more people, more things to do, but most of the places seemed to be closed, except for a couple of clubs with music thumping behind the shuttered or blackened windows and those places made him too nervous. But Jungle Books looked nice and inviting and the first time he'd walked in he felt really calm and at home. It looked like somebody took good care of the place and it smelled like coffee and fresh cookies and he was ready to move in and never leave. Then, of course, he'd met Stella and thought she was really something special and she was so nice to him that he felt like she must like him at least a little bit.

Mostly, while he was at the cafe, he'd try to sit real still and listen to Stella talk to the other girl. Unfortunately she didn't really seem to say much personal stuff. It was mostly just work-related things. Pretty boring to Clint, really, although he did like listening to the sound of her voice. So anyway he was left with having to fill in her personal life. He imagined she was probably still in college or possibly recently graduated. He wondered what she was studying. Probably literature or art or something but that could just be because the cafe was also a bookstore and it made sense. He supposed it could just have easily been something like nursing or education. She radiated a kind of warmth and seemed nurturing. He knew if he spent enough time around her she would see what a good guy he was. All she needed to do was give him a chance and he was sure she would see it.

Tonight could be the night, he mused as he followed her out of downtown.

She really needed a better car. A girl like that . . . it wasn't safe for her to be driving around downtown in a car that wasn't a hundred percent safe. Granted, it looked better than his car, but he could take care of himself if he broke down. Maybe they could trade in both cars for a better one. He didn't have a job to go to, so she could use it the most to get to school and work and whatever. He was okay with that. He'd need to stay at home and tend to Ma anyway and he was sure Stella wouldn't mind stopping at the store on her way home to pick up some groceries.

He wondered what their first meal together would be like. He didn't have enough money to take her out to any place fancy so he'd probably have to prepare something at home. The stove was kind of on the fritz at the moment, so he'd probably just have to put together something real simple like ham sandwiches and Doritos. Sounded great to him. He hoped she wasn't a drinker. He couldn't stand the stuff. He figured she probably wasn't or else she'd be tending bar and making way more tip money than she did at the cafe. A girl who looked like her wouldn't have any problems getting hired at a bar, but she wasn't like that. She wasn't trashy. He knew all those lady bartenders were only bartenders until the bar closed. Then, of course, they became little more than prostitutes, going home with any drunk guy who had a little bit of money. Not that Clint had ever been in a bar. Ma had told him all he needed to know about girls like that.

He expected Stella to turn onto the highway and head out to one of Dayton's suburbs but she turned onto the state route. This was the way he took to get home. It passed through one of the worst sections of the city before turning into farm country. He'd be really surprised if she lived in a bad part of town. Truthfully, he was a little surprised she didn't live downtown like her co-worker. There was something about Stella that seemed really . . . cutting edge. That's what he was thinking. Stylish.

Maybe she lived in the same town as him. Wouldn't that be something? It would certainly make things a lot easier. And they could probably see each other a lot more. Clint found his hopes rising. Plus, if she lived in the same town, they'd have all kinds of things to talk about. Maybe they'd even gone to the same high school. Clint doubted they'd had any of the same teachers. It had been twenty years since he'd gone there and Stella couldn't be more than five years out of high school. Plus, he imagined it wasn't the traumatic experience for her that it was for him.

He continued following her, closing his distance somewhat. It had been so long since he'd started following her that he felt pretty safe. She wouldn't know it was him. And, hey, so what if she did? This was the same way he went home every night anyway. It was almost like he wasn't following her at all. Just going home.

When she turned onto his road, he started to get a little nervous. No. Nervous wasn't really the right word. Curious was more like it. He felt like it would be absolutely impossible for the object of his obsession to live on the same road as him, especially since there were only like four or five houses on the entire stretch and he was pretty sure he at least kind of knew who most of them were. Like, he was pretty sure he would have known if Stella lived on his road. There had been a really pretty girl who lived a couple houses down from him. Clint had many many times found himself behind the school bus that dropped her off from the high school. And, it was kind of funny, because once the school bus pulled away, his car almost always stalled and he couldn't seem to get it started again until the pretty girl had made it almost all the way up her driveway. But then she'd gotten a car and eventually gone away to college and sometimes Clint still missed her.

Actually, they were passing that house now, which meant they were really close to Clint's. He took a long drink of his sweet Venom, his heart pounding, his ears ringing.

Maybe this was a bad idea. Maybe he should swing into his driveway and not continue following Stella. He wasn't really tired, but Ma was probably wondering where he was and he didn't know how much farther away Stella lived.

Then he thought maybe he should speed up and overtake Stella's car, run her off the road. It wouldn't be hard to do that and get her up to the house. He could even come back for her car. He'd probably be able to get away with it. There was virtually no traffic on this road, especially at this hour, and the cops never came out here. He'd never done anything like that before.

As tempting as it seemed, he'd missed his chance.

Stella, without even using her turn signal, had turned into his drive-way.

Clint slowed to a stop.

He needed to think.

FOUR

Stella had followed Clint home from his last visit to Jungle Books. Maybe if he didn't creepily sit in his car waiting for her and Jaime to lock the door, she wouldn't have been able to do that. But, predictably, he had, and now she was here. She was pretty sure that was his car way down there on the road. She thought he would have been overjoyed at the prospect of having her at his house. Must be more overwhelmed than overjoyed, at the moment. He'd get used to it.

It was a shame things hadn't worked out with Ronald, but she just couldn't take it anymore. The problem wasn't Ronald per se, it was his kids. His adult kids. Mainly Brian, his son. True, Ronald had become a little more handsy than usual lately, a little more persistent, but less than a week after Brian had moved back home following his failed first marriage, Stella knew it was time to move on. Take a desperate older man like Ronald and he was too close to the situation to fully take it in. Couldn't see the forest for the trees, as the old cliché goes. He could fully believe the fantasy. Not that the fantasy encompassed much more than what was between her legs. A trophy wife who was younger than his son would have undoubtedly made him a standout among his friends, of which he did not have many. Not that Stella would have, in a million years, married the schmuck. Or, for that matter, ever even let him fuck her. Still, she wished she could have strung him along a little more before Brian had put an end to it. Brian had, in a sense, created this emergency situation. Ronald had a daughter, too, named Karen. But they didn't talk about Karen. He'd been adamant about that. There were no photos of her anywhere in the house. Karen had even seemingly been removed from the family photo albums Stella had snooped through. The first time she had ever even heard the name was when she had asked about the old Fiero in the garage. It didn't seem like something Ronald would, in a million years, have ever purchased. At least not for himself.

"Who's car is that?" Stella had asked.

"Karen's," Ronald had said after a very pregnant pause.

"Who's Karen?"

"We don't talk about her." Stella had seen a look in Ronald's eyes that wasn't hurt, exactly. Just a hollowed out, deeply inward expression.

So, okay, he didn't talk about Karen.

Why wasn't Mr. Stalky coming up the driveway?

For one fleeting second she imagined him calling the cops out of some sense of alarm but quickly laughed it off. Dude was wearing pants made out of toilet paper. He wasn't calling the cops.

She checked her phone.

One text from Ronald that said, "What time will you be home to-night?" and one from Brian, "I hope we can hang out again tonight."

That word—"again"—made it feel like this was all her fault. She had been bored and wanted someone closer to her own age to talk to and Brian had been there and desperate and they'd done just that—hung out—exactly one time. It was stupid. She knew how desperate divorced men were. Stella didn't want to obsess upon Karen but thought if she could get a couple drinks in Brian—not at all a challenge, it turned out— she could get him to talk about his sister. Again, she was met with the same response from Brian as she'd gotten from Ronald. "We don't talk about her." After a couple more drinks—again, not a big challenge—she finally got him to say, "Karen's in jail right now, okay?" And after yet a couple more drinks—only a problem because he became nearly impossible to be around—he'd made it clear to Stella if she wanted him to talk about Karen, she would need to give him something she wasn't willing to give. She hoped her gag of revulsion wasn't that noticeable.

She knew she was now making the right decision.

Soon the texts would become calls and then they would stop altogether. Probably when Ronald decided to stop paying for the extra phone line. Didn't really matter. She had about another month left. One glance at the darkened shack in front of her told her this new guy wasn't going to be able to pay any additional cell phone bills. If he even had one himself.

She took a deep breath and decided to familiarize herself with her future husband. Always a future husband and never a, you know, *actual* husband.

She got out of the car and surveyed the surroundings. The moon was large, not completely full, and a security lamp buzzed high over her car, moths frenetically swimming around the yellow pool of light it created. She took a look around her while breathing in the night smells. Clean outdoor country air. That was important. She didn't know how long she'd be here but felt like outdoor walks might have to become a new ritual. *Hobby,* she corrected herself. Ritual sounded too . . . Well, it practically sounded like a crime these days. She tried to embrace this new turn her life had taken, this new version of herself. Like a poet disappearing into a mountain cabin to reinvent herself. That's what kept life fresh and new: reinvention. She could already see how the wildness of this rural setting could replace the clipped sterility of Ronald's sprawling, posh suburban home—everything neat, neat, neat. She took another deep breath, as though she could absorb this new location's essence and create a mental map of the next however many days. There was an underlying odor she found almost putrid. Not quite gag inducing but she thought it might be if she were any closer to the source. Probably just a septic tank. Or, given the overall rustic nature of the place, it could be coming from an outhouse. So much for clean outdoor air.

She threw another glance toward the car on the road.

Why was he just sitting there?

Maybe he'd decided to keep it stealth and come up on foot.

She looked for any sign of movement along the driveway or among the fields to either side of it.

Nothing.

She began walking toward the house. The pungent smell grew stronger. Maybe she'd made a terrible mistake.

All she had to do was think of poor Ronald, sitting in his leather chair, pumping his sad old man cock and saying, "A man's got needs, Stella," or the now even more impending and menacing threat of Brian trapping her against a wall after a couple of drinks, his hardness pressing against her stomach as he slurred out, "I'm gonna fuck you tomorrow. This life you been living isn't free. I'm gonna teach you what it's like to pay for something," and she once again convinced herself she'd made the right choice. Maybe not the best choice, but the right choice.

The porch steps creaked under her meager weight. The paint wasn't just peeling off the house and porch, it looked like it had blown away completely at least a decade ago.

She put her hand on the knob to the front door. People used to say no one in the country bothered locking their doors but she guessed things had changed. She no longer looked at people who lived on farms as doing so to escape the fast pace of city life. Now she saw them as creepy paranoiacs girding themselves from the outside world with land and guns and vicious dogs. People who seemed more apt to call their place of residence a compound than a homestead.

The knob turned freely.

And some of them, thankfully, knew they were dirt poor and didn't have anything worth stealing.

The smell that smacked her in the face like a palpable thing could have been all the protection they needed.

She was not confronted by a snarling dog or a vicious yokel wielding a shotgun.

Just that stench.

Her stomach lurched and she swallowed rapidly to keep from throwing up.

She flipped a light switch and nothing happened.

She brought her phone out and clicked the flashlight on. She scanned it over a mountain of mail ascending from a table beside the door. She flipped through it. Her future husband was probably not Alma Mackey, whose name appeared on most of the envelopes. It looked like Alma Mackey was terrible at paying bills. Then she found a pink postcard from *Hustler* Magazine. It read "We Miss You" and was addressed to Clint Mackey (or Current Resident).

Clint Mackey. She thought about it. The name fit. She would never think of him as Mr. Stalky again.

She wondered who Alma was.

Couldn't be his wife. The man who had come to the cafe for the past couple of months did not have a wife. No way.

So maybe it was his mom.

Stella's tension dissolved somewhat.

If some old woman wandered out and asked what Stella was doing in her house, she'd just tell her she was looking for Clint. Stella knew she was pretty, knew Clint was a monster, and felt like her future mother-in-law would be more than happy that someone like Stella showed an interest in someone like Clint.

Holding the phone in front of her, shining its bright light all around, Stella wandered deeper into the house, that smell getting worse and worse. She paused to pull her shirt up over her nose and mouth, catching a hint of coffee and girl sweat, only slightly masking the atrocious smell she seemed to be walking right into. The path became narrower and narrower until she didn't have any other choice but to follow it. The stench was now so intense she considered turning around and going back from whence she had come, but just when she didn't think she could take another breath, the light on her phone captured a bed and its contents.

She was pretty sure she'd found Alma.

She turned to run back out of the house, gagged on her own bile, doubled over, and vomited on the unidentifiable debris of the path.

Clint now stood a few feet in front of her.

"Stella . . . What are you doing in my house?" he said.

"Oh, Clint, honey," she said. "I think I'm sick."

FIVE

Clint took a drink of his Venom and poured a little in the glass of water he'd poured for Stella. He didn't know what would be better for a sick person—water or energy drink—so he decided to do a little of both. He'd led her to one of the upstairs bedrooms. Sometimes his memory surprised him. He couldn't remember the last time he'd seen the staircase but, once he knocked down the wall of old *National Geographics* and compacted IGA bags, it revealed itself like some hidden chamber. The upstairs was remarkably less cluttered. Like Ma had just gotten too lazy to go upstairs and tried to block it from view so she could forget it even existed.

He guided Stella to an old bed. She complained about it being hot and he went to open a window and the whole thing fell out of the fixture.

"Opened a window for ya," he said. "It should cool down soon."

Clint was a little confused but he didn't want to think too much about it. After all, it made perfect sense. His gut had been totally right all along. Stella did have a thing for him. So what was there to be confused about something that made perfect sense?

He took another slug of his Venom.

They'd probably be fucking in no time.

He hoped Ma hadn't seen her.

If so, he'd just tell her it was a social worker.

Ma wasn't too quick on her feet these days. Her brain was probably filled with cancer or Alzheimer's or something. Worms, maybe.

A scream rang out from upstairs and Clint grabbed Stella's drink and headed up.

He found her with her legs pulled up to her chest, pressed into the corner the bed was in. She had her phone out, shining it on something moving on the far side of the room.

"What the fuck is it?" she asked.

"That's just Gobby," Clint said. "He's a critter."

"What kind of . . . critter is it?"

"Gobby's an old possum. She won't hurt ya."

Clint noticed the movement didn't stop with Gobby.

"Looks like Gobby's multiplied," he said.

"I can't rest in here. Not with those things."

"I made you a drink."

He handed the drink to her. If he'd known she was going to be here, he would have tried to get hold of something that would knock her out. He didn't even have any liquor in the house. God was he stupid. And now he'd given her a diluted energy drink. That was only going to keep her awake.

She took a sip and made a face.

"What's wrong with it?" she asked.

"It's water and Venom. I mean, that's the name of an energy drink, not real venom. I mean, it ain't gonna hurt ya. I thought it might make ya feel better. There's vitamins in it."

"You're so thoughtful," she said. "Do you think you can do something about . . .?"

"Gobby? I guess."

Clint found a large sheet that didn't have too many holes in it, gathered up Gobby and her kin, took them all out into the yard, beat them to death with a large board, and burned them in the fire pit. When he went back upstairs Stella was sleeping and when he tried to play with her tits she woke up and told him she wasn't ready for that yet so Clint had to go downstairs and spend some time with Ma.

Things continued in a similar vein for the next two weeks.

It started with Stella complaining about Ma. Ma had always warned him about this. Said every woman was a jealous woman.

"I think that's what's making me sick," Stella said as they looked in on Ma's bedroom.

"It ain't a that," Clint said. "That's my ma."

"Sweetie, your ma's dead." Stella placed a hand on his bare arm and something inside him folded and melted. He was pretty sure he would do anything she asked him to. "Looks like she's been dead a really long time."

It hurt for him to hear this but he guessed he had to admit it was true. Coming to terms with this grim acceptance wasn't the worst of it, though. He had known Ma wasn't right for some time. She wasn't the same woman who had raised him to be the man he was today. He probably should have called someone to take her away a long time ago.

But there were other things to consider. Like her social security check. Financially, that was the only thing keeping him afloat and he was pretty well aware his idea of floating would look like drowning to most people. And there was the matter of what she demanded of him on a nearly daily basis. Although he was pretty sure once Stella started putting out Ma would be so jealous she wouldn't let him come anywhere near that sacred place again.

"I'm afraid you're wrong," he said.

"*This*," Stella pointed at Ma, "is not a living person. *This* is a rotting corpse."

"She ain't doin too good but she's still alive."

"What makes you say that?"

"She talks to me."

Stella looked at her phone. "Okay. Well, I have to go to work. I don't want to have to make you choose but I'm telling you I cannot live with that smell."

"I'll take care of it. I just don't want you talkin about her anymore."

Clint thought Stella would at least kiss him goodbye or something but she just lightly punched him on his biceps and said, "I'll be home around eleven. You know what you need to do."

Then she left Clint all alone to deal with this dilemma, which he was determined to do. He tried spraying Ma down with some household cleanser and then showered her with some knockoff Febreze. The commercials made it sound like it could make anything smell better. But it only seemed to make it worse. He gave himself a Febreze treatment and then went outside to get some fresh air and came back in. Nope. It was like his brief foray into scented toilet paper. It made things smell like flowers and shit instead of just shit. Still not good. He thought about just moving her outside or even into a different room. One upstairs maybe. He was pretty sure smells rose, like heat. But he wanted to make Stella happy and, hey, he got it. She was jealous. She knew he'd have to divide his time between her and Ma as long as the old battle-axe was still around. It wasn't that he didn't love his Ma but he had to admit she would be in the way. Besides, Stella's room was upstairs too, so that would never work. He told himself that whatever happened to Ma, he would always carry her in his heart.

He did some sawing on her to extricate her sacred place—she'd told him it was sacred because that's where *he* had come from—and then he disposed of her in much the same way he had Gobby and her little ones. He was pretty sure he could hear her yelling and screaming at him the entire time and he had to keep reminding himself what Stella had said. This was a corpse and corpses didn't talk. He shoved some paper towel into his ears but it didn't cut out her nagging.

"See," he told himself, "it's all in your head."

Once the body was burning all right, he wrapped the pelvis in an old Family Dollar bag and stashed it under the bed.

He would have thought Stella would be ecstatic after he'd performed this feat but she seemed to become even more demanding. She wanted this room cleaned and that room cleaned. She asked him to remove the stack of gym mats from the bathtub. And she still complained about the smell. So, every day when she went off to work, he was left cleaning the house just to keep her happy. He was so exhausted by the end of the day he didn't even have the energy to visit her at Jungle Books or spend quality time with Ma, no matter how much Venom he drank. And, yes, of course he knew he'd burned Ma up in the fire so he saw it more as spending time with her spirit, like going to a graveside or something. It just so happened that her spirit was a pelvis and her idea of quality time was him stripping down and making her happy. Not that he'd been able to do that. Never had.

Stella didn't reward him in any way when she came back from work. She'd made it very clear early on that touching her was off limits but she wouldn't even talk to him anymore, not that they had ever really talked much to begin with. She just came home, took a shower, put on a very modest sweat suit, and went to her room where he imagined she lay around with that stupid phone glued to her hand. He couldn't even watch her without her saying it was creepy and weird. He wanted to tell her she could stay here as long as she wanted as long as he could look at her anytime he wanted and, okay, sometimes maybe also touch himself while he did it. But he couldn't even imagine doing that. She seemed so sensitive. He knew she would just pack up her stuff and take off if he did anything like that. This was all starting to make his previous life look more appealing and he was glad Ma had told him to extricate her spirit from her body. That at least made it feel like he had a bit of both lives, even if neither one of them was too great.

SIX

For some reason it had never even occurred to Stella to try gaslighting one of her hosts into suicide. Then again, she'd never found herself in a situation as isolated and dismal as this.

Like, if she had just convinced poor old Ronald to end things, people would have noticed.

People like Brian, who had abruptly stopped texting and calling her. The final few texts had seemed more concerned than horny or angry. It wasn't until he showed up at Jungle Books that she realized the anger was still very much there.

He strolled in at the tail end of a lunch rush, spotted her, and calmly took his place third deep in line. Stella thought about abandoning the counter and leaving Joad to deal with him but Joad wasn't very assertive and got overwhelmed easily and this sometimes caused him to pee his pants and have to go home. Besides, ever since taking his place in line, Brian had affixed some kind of predatory death stare on her and she imagined that stare following her to wherever she tried disappearing. It didn't matter. Living like she lived, she'd experienced all manner of uncomfortable situations. She could deal with it.

"Brian," she said as he stepped up to the counter, rapping his knuckles in a militant drumming fashion on the faux granite surface. "What can I get you?"

"How about some fucking sympathy," he said. "I don't want anything. Just wanted to see for myself that you're alive. Now I can let Pops know. He's worried himself so sick we're thinking about putting him in hospice."

"I don't know what you want me to say."

He rapidly knocked his knuckles against the counter before pointing his index finger a couple inches from Stella's face.

"Hospice," he said. "That's pretty fucking sick."

"Maybe you should go."

He sprang forward like he was going to leap across the counter. Stella took a startled step back and tried to remember where the large sandwich knife was.

"This isn't over," Brian said. "I know what you're doing."

Then he turned to stomp out of the store.

Stella turned to Joad, noticing the dark stain on his skinny jeans before anything else.

"Jesus Christ, Joad," she said.

"I'm *sorry*. My parents never taught me to deal with stress."

"Get out from behind the counter. I'll call Jaime."

Jaime said she could be there within an hour and without Joad's assistance the time passed quickly, leaving Stella no time to think about things.

When she did finally have a quiet moment she found her thoughts going to Clint rather than Brian.

That morning she had told a completely nude Clint that she'd like for him to clean out the refrigerator before she returned this evening.

"I just don't know how much longer I can keep doin this," he'd said before taking a slug of his energy drink, which he now decanted into a dirty glass before cutting with water. He said this was to make them stretch further since he didn't have time to go to the store anymore.

"What do you mean you can't keep doing this? Doing what?" she asked.

"All this cleanin. All these chores. I ain't had to do shit like this for a long time and I'm just wore out. Ma never kept after me the way you do."

"This is what normal people do, baby. They pick up after themselves. They don't live like animals."

"Ain't nothin normal happenin here."

"What do you mean?"

"We're supposed to be girlfriend and boyfriend, ain't we?"

"Of course. That's why I'm here." She swallowed, stole a quick glance at his filthy penis, and said, "I knew I wanted to be with you the first time I saw you."

"Same here," he said. "The problem is you been here a long time and we ain't never been together. Ain't never had relations. If I'm runnin around turnin this place into the goddamn Taj Mahal, I expect a little reward, you know?"

She tried her best to look hurt. "I thought . . . I thought me being here was the reward." She let her eyes drift up and down his body. "No. It's okay. I get it now. That's why you're always naked, isn't it? Because you're just waiting to fuck me, right? You just want me to come home from a hard day's work, walk in the door, and throw off my clothes so we can get right to the fucking, huh? *Fucking* is all you think about, isn't it?" She tried her best to make that word—fucking—sound more like a disease than a desirous act.

"That ain't it at all," he said. "I haven't been able to find my clothes and ain't had time to make more."

"It makes me feel really cheap," she said. "Really objectified." He'd never admit he didn't know what that word meant.

"I just need a day off every now and then," he said. "Sometimes I think I'd rather just kill myself than live like this."

Stella took a step toward him and gently placed a hand on his cheek.

"I need to get to work," she said. "Can we talk about this when I get home?"

"I guess," he said. "And I'll try to get that refrigerator cleaned."

"And maybe try finding some clothes? A lot of girls find mystery very seductive."

"I'll see what I can do. I wanna be perfect for ya."

"Oh, Clint . . . you're *so close.*"

Now Stella again thought about what Clint's death might mean for her.

SEVEN

As soon as Stella left, Clint went into a frenzy. He was naked and erect and his brain felt too full, like all the contents of the house were suddenly trying to crowd inside his skull. He went into Ma's room and dug out the pelvis. Maybe most of her body was buried but this part was still here, the most important part, the part from which he had come. And if **Ma** was so dead, why did she still talk to him? After throwing the pelvis onto the bed and furiously mounting it, the next couple of minutes were a whirlwind of exertion and conversation, his Ma whispering encouraging words until Clint was spent and collapsed beside her.

Then the needling began.

"You never can satisfy me," Ma said.

Clint huffed and hopped out of bed.

"At least you used to try a little more often. Now . . ."

"I can't, Ma. Not every day. You know I found someone. What if she comes home and she's ready? I only got about one load every couple days. Ain't like when I was younger. I need to be able to get it up for her. That's what you always wanted. Little ones runnin around. You said I was a wasted shot and the only way I could be worth it to you was if I was to make more."

"Then what are you waiting for?"

"Stella's real special, Ma. I didn't think I'd ever find no one like that."

"She's a cunt, Clint. A hole. You need to put us in that hole. Make her one of us."

"I don't want you talkin bout Stella anymore. You got that? From now on, we don't talk about her. Why don't you just let me do it my way? I got you in one ear tellin me to do this and that and I got her in the other ear. I can't do everything! Why don't you just let me do things my way for once?"

"Because your way is always a disappointment."

Clint couldn't listen to this anymore. He wrapped what was left of Ma up in the bag and shoved her back under the bed.

That bag . . . it didn't smell too good. Clint didn't know if it was because he'd been cleaning more, making the rest of the house smell good, or what but . . . he didn't know if he'd be able to stomach unwrapping Ma from that bag again. He went into the bathroom and scrubbed the slime and stench from his cock and balls. For the first time in a long time, he thought maybe this wasn't normal.

Then he went down to the kitchen and emptied out everything in the refrigerator and took it all outside and threw it over the hill behind the house. The fridge was already starting to smell better but there was still a lot of work to do. He sprayed the cleaner in it and went through at least ten old rags and when he was finished he was pretty damn sure it was sparkling. He felt really proud of himself. And proud of Stella for noticing the refrigerator needed cleaning. Ma had never pointed that out to him. Ma didn't ever want him to throw anything away. Just wanted to surround herself with piles of shit like a creepy old trash goblin.

Clint stood in front of the refrigerator, opening and closing the door, surprised every time at how clean it was. He really had done a good job.

He had no idea what time it was but felt like it must be getting close to Stella coming back. He was tired and dirty but didn't have enough time to take a bath or shower.

He sprayed himself with the kitchen cleaner and used the cleanest of the rags to give himself a wipe down. Then he chugged some energy drink and felt a lot better about things.

He wanted to surprise Stella and hoped he had enough time to put something together.

EIGHT

Stella was not a black widow. For a couple of reasons. The mystique of the female black widow is that she fucks and kills. Stella did not fuck. Never had and never would. Her stance on this was unwavering. She had the same steely resolve as the child of an alcoholic who vows to never take her first drink. Secondly, she did not kill. Of the men and women who had hosted her over the past several years, not one of them had died while she was there. That was never the point. It was about the game. The exchange. The experience. She wanted their attention. Felt like they *needed* her attention. The free room and board was more like a bonus.

The life of the working poor was not sustainable. Even if she were to split rent with other people, that still left a car payment or, at the very least, insurance, food, healthcare, etc. There just wasn't enough. It was like one of those casino games where you might win a little but would always lose overall.

Unless you walked away.

That's how she saw the life she had chosen to live. A walking away. Not giving up. Not at all. Separating.

And by walking away from the conventional life of a struggling twenty-something, she had exposed herself to worlds she never would have known existed. She had friends whose lives were lived on some depressing loop. They divided their time between work and school and studying, trying to fit in a boyfriend or a girlfriend who could ideally help them pay for things but always ended up being way more of a headache than a help. All of this to put way too much money on their credit cards to do something during their modicum of free time that advertisers convinced them was fun. They all acted like they had no control over their own lives.

That was one thing Stella felt like she had.

Control.

Someone once said that knowledge was power and if Stella was the only one who knew the rules to the game she was playing, that was power.

But never had she considered using that power to hurt one of her hosts.

The only reason she was even thinking about it now was because of what Clint had said about killing himself.

Would that really be such a bad thing?

He didn't work. He just received a couple checks, like magic, at the beginning of the month. One was for him. The other was for his dead mother. Since Alma was still getting checks, it only stood to reason that Clint would continue getting checks if something happened to him. She wasn't naive enough to think it would last forever, but Clint being out of the picture while everything else remained the same seemed like less of a burden.

Of course, cashing dead people's social security checks was a crime and that was something she'd always been very conscientious about. She'd seen far too many young people handicap themselves before they could even really begin living life. One could argue that how she'd been living was morally objectionable but the law was what mattered and she had never broken that.

She shook the idea away.

There was no way someone who couldn't even find his clothes could muster the knowledge and the energy to kill himself.

She pulled into the driveway, filled with equal parts dread and amusement.

She checked her phone and sighed before opening the car door. Sometimes she didn't even really know if it was worth it or not. With people like Ronald, people who were older and more stable, it was easy to convince herself she was living in the lap of luxury. It was easier to enjoy herself. She'd even had friends over when she lived there. But this thing with Clint . . . It made her feel like it would almost be worth it to rent some random studio apartment in the bad part of town. Then she thought about the money in her bank account and knew it wouldn't be worth it. She had a plan and she had to stick to it.

Besides, she reminded herself, this was only temporary.

Not just the thing with Clint but the whole game in general.

Just a few more years and she'd be about where she'd want to be financially.

Maybe she'd go to a bar tomorrow after work or something. Try to find someone who could provide her with a more comfortable life. Maybe she'd chat some people up on Facebook tonight. She didn't have to stay here just because Clint was the first person to come along.

Christ, how she dreaded going back into that house.

Minus twelve half-siblings ranging in age from two to seventeen and a sharp-tongued inattentive mother, it was just too much like going home. The piles of trash, the smell of things rotting, the all-pervasive feel of abuse and neglect.

Only temporary, she told herself as she got out of the car and began the dread-filled walk to the front door.

Just like Ronald's turned out to be only temporary, spoiled by the arrival of Brian and the looming specter of "We don't talk about" Karen.

She opened the door to find Clint slouched in an awkward way in the foyer, kind of leaning against one of the walls like he was posing for something.

"I was wonderin when you'd get back," he said.

"What are you wearing?" While she was happy he'd at least clothed himself, it looked like he'd fashioned a shirt and pants out of old yellow and black Dollar General bags.

"I still couldn't find no clothes so I had to make this. You like it?"

He opened up his arms, his new outfit crinkling loudly.

"Whatever," she said. "I'm going upstairs to take a bath and go to bed. It was brutal at work today." Other than the visit from Brian, this wasn't true at all, but if she had to stand here looking at a grown man wearing Dollar General bags for another second, she was pretty sure she'd either scream or try to rip his eyes out.

"Don't you want to see the refrigerator? I cleaned it real good."

"I'll look tomorrow." She'd already started for the stairs.

"Don't I get a kiss goodnight?"

Stella didn't bother to respond.

NINE

Clint couldn't believe it. He wanted to yank off the outfit he'd worked at least an hour on—it was so hot and scratchy anyway. Then he wanted to go into Ma's room and take his frustrations out on her until he remembered the smell of that bag and again had the thought that Stella was ruining everything.

He had to remind himself she wasn't. He liked looking at her. He liked having her here. He liked the way she smelled. She listened to him when she was actually around. Or, at least he thought she did. As much as Ma ever did, anyway. She was a lot younger than him. He had to remind himself of that. People her age were able to listen and scroll through their phones at the same time. They even had a word for it. What was it? Multitasking? Just because Clint wasn't able to focus on more than one thing at a time didn't mean Stella wasn't. And she probably just never really responded because she didn't have much to say. He was clearly older and more experienced than she was. So what if she made him do things like clean out the refrigerator and burn Ma in the yard? She wanted a nice house. He reckoned most women did. Weren't those things he needed to do anyway? Not every woman was like Ma. Not every woman wanted to just let things pile up.

He loved Stella. That's what it was. It was a feeling he was unfamiliar with. It was possible to love a woman who didn't also give birth to you. That was maybe even what most normal people did and he recognized how tough that was. It was love at first sight, he supposed. Not the first time it had ever happened for him but it was the first time it had ever been reciprocated. And since they planned to get married, that pretty much made Stella his fiancé.

Maybe he'd make her a glass of water and Venom and take it up to her.

He started for the kitchen before hearing the sound of shattering glass outside.

He rushed to the door and flung it open in time to see a car rolling down the driveway in the murk of the night, its lights off.

Clint's heart raced but he wanted to make sure the car was gone before he went outside. What if whoever that was decided to come back?

Stella's feet pounded on the stairs behind him.

"What the hell was that?" she said.

"There was a car," Clint said.

"What?"

"I saw a car going down the driveway."

"Fuck." She slipped her shoes back on and went out to the porch. She turned to Clint and said, "You coming or not?"

He looked quickly around for his own shoes but didn't see them. He followed Stella out into the night, his outfit almost deafening in the quiet.

Stella marched toward her car and he noticed her shoulders drop as she got closer to it.

"What is it?" he asked.

"Just stay back." Her eyes still on her car, she held a flattened palm up to him.

Of course he couldn't stay back. She looked distressed and he needed to be beside her in her time of need. He began walking toward her, rustling loudly.

Now she turned to him. "Clint," she said sharply. "I mean it."

"It ain't too bad, is it?"

"Yes," she said. "It's really fucking bad."

As he moved closer, he expected and therefore wasn't surprised to see one or more of her windows shattered. He wasn't even really surprised by the slashed tires. What surprised him was the dead man in the passenger seat.

TEN

Up to this point, Stella had felt she was playing the game flawlessly. Now it was apparent she had made a wrong move. What left her confused was that her wrong move was currently in the passenger seat of her car, the shattered ruin of his left eye socket indicating that he was most probably dead.

Brian.

Her first thought was suicide but the self-importance of that idea prevented her from exploring it further. That was naturally followed by her next thought that if there was a dead guy in her car and that dead guy happened to be a murder victim then she might be in immediate danger.

Clint, however, was making it incredibly difficult to think at all.

He stood next to her, his trembling making his plastic bag costume or outfit or whatever crinkle like he was a radio tuned to a channel playing nothing but static.

"Oh my god," Clint said. "Do you know who that is?"

Stella was too busy trying to calm her own nerves to also deal with Clint's questions.

"Clint . . . baby . . . can you please give me some space?"

"Did someone kill him? It looks like someone killed him."

"I'm trying to think. You either need to move away from me or take off your clothes."

"You want me to take off my clothes? You're finally ready?"

This last question dumbfounded Stella so thoroughly it actually diverted her attention from the dead body long enough for her to look at Clint and say, "You're not fucking serious, are you?"

He didn't answer. Just stood there trembling in the darkness, the moon full and pus-yellow overhead. The only thing she could hear was the crinkling of his outfit.

"Just go inside and have some energy drink. I'll deal with this."

She thought he would protest more. Maybe even hoped he would. She didn't want to be alone. Instead he said, "Yeah. I'll let you deal with it. It's gonna be real hard work and I been workin hard all day. Workin hard with no reward! Never a break! Never a reward! No treats for Clint!"

He turned and crinkled back into the house, clearly in the middle of some personal crisis she had no interest in understanding.

Stella welcomed the silence. She needed to think about what she was going to do.

She couldn't call the police. There would be way too much explaining to do. And when she couldn't even begin to figure out how this had happened, she couldn't possibly form the necessary, logical explanations.

She moved close enough to the car to see Brian's hands and look around the seat and floorboard of her car to make sure she couldn't see a gun. She wouldn't have thought she was important enough to Brian for him to kill himself over but he was a late middle-aged guy with a heavy drinking problem, a disastrous life, and no real options, so it wasn't that far-fetched to think he'd turned her into something more meaningful than she was in his dark hours of loneliness. She had no idea how light opioid abuse and extreme self-delusion affected one's thinking.

But, if not suicide, who would kill Brian?

The only one with any motive she could remotely see was Ronald but Brian had said he was really sick or in hospice or something. Even if that was a lie, Ronald seemed too old and frail to do something like this. And

Brian was his *son*. Stella couldn't imagine herself being something for Ronald to kill his only son over.

Who did that even leave?

It couldn't have been Clint. He didn't have the time, was completely unaware and uninterested in her immediate past, and seemed genuinely freaked out by the whole incident.

Maybe Karen, but how could she do something like this if she was in jail?

Brian's ex-wife? Maybe she'd been following Brian around. Maybe Brian had been following Stella. Stella could see it, if that were the case. Jealous ex-wife following Brian as he pursued his new interest. But, come on, Brian wasn't the type of guy you committed crimes for. He was the type of guy you were glad to be rid of.

A new panic rose within Stella.

What if she had perfectly answered her own question?

Brian was the type of guy you were glad to be rid of.

He had kids with his ex-wife, meaning she could never truly be rid of him unless . . .

Unless he was dead.

And if she *had* spent any time following Brian around, Stella would probably seem like the easiest person to pin something like that on. Stella and her crazy, poor new boyfriend knocking off Brian to try and get at Ronald's fortune or just to get Brian out of her hair.

Fuck.

She expected an explosion of sirens and lights at any moment.

What she got was something a lot quieter but a lot more disturbing.

A pale shape moved toward her from the darkness.

It was Ronald.

He was holding a gun.

And he was naked.

ELEVEN

"Stella?" He seemed confused.

It was still hard for her to see him shooting Brian. Couldn't imagine him shooting *anyone*. He was a retired English professor who'd spent his retirement volunteering at a peace museum until he became physically unable. Nevertheless, she found herself moving to the opposite side of the car, trying to put a bit of steel in between them.

"Ronald?" she said. "What are you doing here?"

"I don't . . ."

He raised the hand holding the gun to scratch his forehead and part of Stella wanted to reach out and take the gun from him and tell him not to do that.

"Put the gun down, Ronald."

"I don't . . . why do I have a gun?"

He continued moving toward her, coming further into the yellow pool of the security lamp, his balls swinging between his thighs. Blood oozed from a spot on his head and his body was covered in bruises and scratches.

"You are Stella, aren't you? One of my prettiest students. Where am I?"

Stella had never been one of his students. She'd never even been to college, but she knew there was no use in explaining any of this to him.

"Yeah, Ronald. My name's Stella. You're at my new place."

"But . . . you live with me."

He looked like he was on the verge of tears and the overall sad sight of him pulled at some long unfelt part of her emotions. Had she done this to him or was it some inevitable part of Alzheimer's or senile dementia, long dormant, finally risen to claim him?

"Not anymore. I live here now."

"Why don't . . .? You could come back. My son's there now. You'd get along real good. He's still in high school though."

Definitely Alzheimer's or something. She didn't have the heart to tell him she'd already met his son and he was one of the biggest assholes on the planet and she *really* didn't want to tell him that his son was dead in her car right now.

"Who brought you here?" she said.

"I don't even know where I am. I want to go home. This place smells like a toilet."

He wasn't even wearing his false teeth, which made him seem even more distant from the Ronald she had known. It had only taken a few weeks for him to go from a well-groomed, respectable elderly man with most of his faculties about him to this confused, wandering crazy person who couldn't even be bothered with clothes or teeth, let alone putting together a stylish outfit. Whatever he had was moving quickly.

"Put the gun down, Ronald."

He stood there as though contemplating her question and she realized she probably should have first reminded him he had a gun in his hand before asking him to put it down. She stepped out from around the car, intending to move toward him and take the gun. For self-defense, if nothing else. She knew Clint didn't own anything like that and could never find it if he did.

Before she could take two steps, she heard the cacophonous crinkling roar of Clint as he streaked out from somewhere behind the house and saw the blur of bright yellow, rendered weird under the outdoor light, as he ran into Ronald, lifting him up and slamming him back to the ground.

"Careful," Stella said. "He's got a gun." But she knew Clint didn't have anything to worry about.

He continued wrestling around with Ronald, although it seemed mostly one-way. The impact had torn Clint's outfit in several places and now he just looked like a guy who had plastic bags taped randomly all over his body. Ronald moaned in pain and misery. Stella imagined nearly every bone in his frail old body was shattered. Clint turned Ronald over onto his stomach and wrenched his arms behind his back.

"Think you can just come here and rape my girl, huh?" Clint said. "Creepin around out in the woods like an old ghoul."

Stella felt paralyzed. She wanted to tell Clint not to hurt him but, really, what was the point? Besides, she was pretty sure Ronald was just a bag of flesh filled with busted chalk by now anyway.

Ronald whimpered and blubbered. Stella moved closer to the two men, but her goal was to find the gun. She had no intent to use it but one of her stepfathers had taught her how to shoot and she felt comfortable around guns. There was, after all, the fact that there was still a killer on the loose and it was possible whoever it was was still in the proximity.

Maybe this had nothing to do with her. Maybe this had something to do with Clint. After all, she didn't know anything about him except that he'd been a sort of laughable stalker who turned out to be living in a dump with the remains of his dead mother. He'd talked about his past, she guessed, but she'd mostly tuned him out while she was busy constructing the narratives of at least three fake identities on MyFace.

No. It had to have something to do with her. Ronald was only the latest in her series of heartbreaks. There hadn't been a ton. Only five since high school, including Ronald. Four men and one woman in total. But she was pretty good at severing ties. She'd made a mistake going back to her job in this case but it was only because Ronald seemed more harmless than all the other ones and she couldn't have imagined spending all day every day at this house with Clint. Regardless, she couldn't imagine any of her exes being capable of murder. They had all been spineless pushovers. That was what allowed her into their lives to orchestrate a sexless, parasitic relationship where she took everything they were willing to give and gave them nothing in return. Besides, they all had something to lose.

Then she saw the one headlight at the end of the driveway racing toward them.

You didn't see many Fieros on the road these days.

It looked like Karen had finally gotten out of jail.

TWELVE

This, Clint told himself, was why he drank so many energy drinks. He'd been pounding them all day. Out of sheer frustration and also because he needed the energy to perform all the tasks Stella set out for him. Now he felt like he had superpowers.

It was with great reluctance that he'd gone back inside at Stella's request. Good thing he hadn't turned his back on her. He hadn't liked the idea of her being out there with that dead body. He knew if he brought it up, Stella would have just accused him of being jealous. So he'd gone inside and watched Stella from the kitchen window as he pounded yet another energy drink. He noticed her attention drawn to something in the darkness and thought maybe he'd heard her say something. Then he'd seen the naked old man and sprang into action. He would have been out there a lot sooner if Ma hadn't stopped him. He thought if he went out the back door he could more easily surprise the man but, just as he reached it, Ma screamed louder than she had in a really long time. He was almost starting to think Stella was right and Ma really was dead. Not just physically dead which, he had to admit, she most assuredly was, but dead of spirit, as well. Completely departed from this earth, leaving behind, even in Clint's head, only memories.

"Don't you go out there!" she screamed.

"I got to, Ma," he said. "Stella's in trouble."

"That cunt *is* the trouble."

"Don't call her that, Ma. She's my fiancé." He hoped he was pronouncing that word right. He didn't think he'd ever spoken it aloud before. "And I *told* you not to talk about her."

"Go on," Ma said. "Go on and get yerself killed."

This gave Clint pause, but only for a second.

"You're just jealous," he said before charging out of the house to the piercing shriek of Ma's high, hysterical laughter.

Then he was running through the too tall grass, his target pale and wraith-like on the far side of the driveway. Clint wished his outfit was a little quieter but the old man didn't seem to hear him or even notice him and when Clint plowed into him, it was like tackling a blanket full of sticks. Panic and rage turned his thoughts red and he was unaware of anything but the energy surging through his body and this squirming old man and the loud crinkling of his outfit.

Stella said something about a gun and Clint hadn't even been aware the man had one. This probably made him look even braver to Stella and if this didn't earn him some kind of reward, he had no idea what would.

He used his raw strength to get the old man over onto his stomach and wrench those arms behind his back. This old guy's skin felt gross and weird and Clint didn't like touching him. He was glad Ma had never let herself get like that. He was pretty sure he'd never have been able to get it up for her if she had. The old guy was whimpering and moaning and the bags were flapping all around Clint from where his energized muscles had apparently expanded so much he'd shredded his clothes just like the Incredible fucking Hulk and he looked all around for Stella but didn't see her and then he was blinded by headlights—no, just one headlight—and he heard the car and just when he thought it sounded like it was going too fast he realized it was headed right for him and he tried to shift his weight to the right but wasn't fast enough and it plowed into him and then he thought he felt some other impact but at that point everything seemed very far away and he tried to open his eyes to look up at the sky one last time but all he could see was Ma and he thought he knew what was happening, thought he'd see her with her arms open, saying something like "Come to your ma. She'll make it all better" or "You're home now, little one, you're home," but all he saw was that sour look on her face and all he heard was a low humiliating laugh coming from her dead withered lips and then his brain hissed out like a candle and all was dark.

THIRTEEN

Stella saw Clint look up just in time for Karen's car to slam into him. The car continued forward, running completely over Ronald, before slamming into Stella's car. It happened so fast Stella didn't have any time to think. She just knew she had to get the fuck out of here. She hadn't backed up that far from her car at the time of impact so she knew Karen had already seen her. Had probably followed her home from work anyway, so she had to know she was here.

Stella's one hope was that the high-speed impact had somehow injured or at least dazed Karen.

But her car door was already opening as Stella broke for the house.

She knew it was stupid to go into the house but if she had any chance of getting far away from this, she was going to need a car. There was no way Clint had his keys on his person. Not in that outfit. She just hoped they were somewhere she could find them. As far as she knew, he hadn't left the property in days, so that wasn't a given.

Before going into the house, she turned to see Karen stalking toward her.

"I see you, little bitch!" she shouted. Her voice was rough, as though she'd spent even her time in prison smoking unfiltered cigarettes and chugging cheap whiskey.

Stella slammed the door behind her. If the knob had a lock, she didn't have time to figure it out, and just hoped that latching the hook in the eye would buy her a couple of minutes. It wouldn't take someone of Karen's size long to barrel through it, she was sure.

What if she had a gun?

Stupid question.

What kind *of gun did she have?* was the more appropriate question.

Stella frantically searched the entrance just inside the doorway and, dear fucking Christ, saw Clint's keys dangling from a nail driven into the drywall. That was, thankfully, a million times easier than she thought it would be.

The sound of Karen throwing herself into the door was enough to snap Stella out of any lingering platitudes she may have had.

She would need to lure Karen deeper into the house so she could escape back out the front door. She'd heard Clint mention a back door but she had never seen one herself.

Stella got moving and started down one of the teetering paths. It was the path she'd taken her first time here, she remembered without a shred of fondness. She turned and knocked a stack of old board games and books over.

That wasn't all.

This particular section of hoard contained some kind of nest.

Apparently Clint had not quite managed to rustle up all of Gobby's kin and at least three angry possums went shooting away from Stella.

She heard the front door finally give and slam into the wall.

Karen was in the house.

The possums were trying to leave the house.

"Holy fuck!" Karen shouted.

As Stella continued down the path, she hoped the possums would delay or frighten Karen, but that wasn't the case.

"Yer some cute ones, all right. I'll play with you uns later. I got a couple big ol nipples you could latch on to."

Then she was kicking through the debris and laughing in her deep growl.

Reaching Ma's room, Stella hit the floor and slid under the bed. She chose this room because it had a window she thought she might be able to get out of if she couldn't make it back to the front door.

Maybe she'd made a bad choice. The smell under the bed was intense and, even with the sense of danger so immediate, she found it impossible not to focus on.

Stella heard Karen thundering down the path. The image of Karen was burned into her brain. She'd never seen so much as a photo and, since Ronald and Brian didn't talk about her, Stella had no idea what to expect. She reminded Stella of her mother, a colossal vortex of attention and resources, a creature built from the need to consume as much as she could before spending her last breath, probably long after she'd outlived everyone she knew. She still couldn't figure out how Ronald could have raised people like Karen and Brian.

"Where you at!" Karen shouted. "I seen you come in here, you little bitch. You might be small but I'll find ya. Then I'm gonna cut off yer head and punish that pussy till it looks like hamburger."

Stella needed to do something but didn't want to make a lot of noise. She wished she'd been able to find the gun. She had Clint's keys she could hold between her fingers—classic self-defense—but guessed Karen had probably been stabbed so many times she wouldn't even notice.

"Gonna scare you out like the fuckin critter you are."

Stella had to bite down her scream at the first gunshot. After the second and the third she was shaking so badly she thought maybe she'd been hit and was in some kind of shock. Her ears rang so loudly she couldn't hear Karen anymore.

She felt around under the bed until her hand landed on what felt like sticky plastic.

Then the bed sank above her, sending her heart racing even faster.

"Bet you and yer new man been fer plenty of rides on this here bed, huh?" Karen's voice sounded like it came from a deceptive distance.

She knows, Stella thought. *She knows exactly where I am and she's just fucking with me.*

Stella's hand went back to the sticky plastic bag. Most importantly, it felt like it contained something hard. It wasn't a gun but she'd have to make it work.

She wrapped her hand around it as best she could.

Now Karen was bouncing on the bed, the bottom of the box spring pressing down on Stella with each heavy descent.

If Karen knew Stella was under here, she wondered if Karen would bother getting to the floor and looking or if she'd just start shooting randomly and hope she hit her.

The mattress pressed down on Stella before releasing. She had to move without thinking. Maybe catch the trashy giant woman off-guard.

Stella was out from under the bed and standing up and swinging whatever it was she held in her hand.

She swung low and hard, aiming for a kneecap or shin.

What she got was so much better.

Judging from the fumes surrounding Karen, she was very very drunk. Apparently, she had not been standing on her feet when bouncing up and down on the bed, but rather her knees. And, after each jump, Stella imagined her going down on her hands and knees, doing everything she could not to fall over. So when Stella swung what she held in her hand, it connected with the center of Karen's fat, mottled face.

Stella didn't stick around to see if that face contained a surprised look or not.

She bounded as best she could over the hoard until she was at the front door and outside. She shifted the thing in her right hand to her left, not bothering to look at it until she was behind the wheel of Clint's car.

The bag had peeled back—presumably from the impact with Karen's face—and she saw what looked like a decayed old pelvic bone.

Despite everything, she still felt some disappointment in Clint. Some men could never cut that cord. Like her endless slew of stepfathers, just lost men looking for a mother, the keeper of a brood.

She let the bone drop to the ground, thankful the car started and she could put as much distance between herself and this house as possible.

She looked in the hazy rearview just long enough to see Karen stumble into the pool of security light. Stella put her head down in anticipation of the possible impact but there probably wasn't any need. Karen was so drunk she couldn't have hit an RV.

Stella didn't even think she took a breath for about another half hour when she was on I-70 and heading west.

She had no real idea where she was going. She'd find a bank tomorrow and take all her money out. It was more than enough to make a fresh start in a new place. And it was all hers. She'd earned every cent of it. She thought maybe she was done playing the game for a while. Not only was the game about the thrill, it was about security. These things could not always live in concert with one another. Taking advantage of people who were not physically intimidating so she could continue to save money—her money—trying to secure her future. Now she realized there weren't really such things as security and safety. Not permanently. Not without some kind of threat. And, as for the thrills, she thought she'd had enough of those to last her a couple lifetimes.

FOURTEEN

Clint didn't really know where he was. It felt like he was just waking up but he wasn't in his bed. It felt like he was outside. He thought he had his eyes open but, since what he was looking at didn't seem to make any sense, he was pretty sure he must be dreaming. There were two cars smashed into each other and something that looked like a pile of rags or maybe a person farther out in the driveway.

Then the most beautiful woman he'd ever seen flooded his vision and he was now certain he was either dreaming or had died and gone to heaven.

He mumbled, "My beautiful injured angel," but something wasn't right with his mouth.

"What?" the angel said.

He tried to say it again.

"Guess yer still alive, huh?" she said.

Yes! he wanted to shout. *Yes! I'm still alive and ready to devote the rest of my life to you!* But he still couldn't move his mouth so well.

The woman bent over him, blood running down her forehead. She placed a large, rough hand around his jaw and wrenched it to the right.

"Try talkin now. You just needed that popped back into place."

"You're . . . so beautiful," was all he could say.

"I ain't gonna argue with ya," she said. "But we got a lotta work to do."

"I can't feel half my body."

"Well, you better start feelin it," she said. She pointed to the crotch of her stained sweatpants and said, "This pussy ain't gonna pound itself."

Clint searched himself for inspiration before his eyes were drawn to an object lying in the perimeter of the security light.

The last piece of Ma.

"I can do it," he said.

DISCOVERING

THE

SHAPE

OF

MY

SKULL

It is Sunday afternoon, late summer, and we laze on the floor. The sun comes in through the window, splashing across the room in a way that seems very conducive to lazing. Jacinda lies on a fuzzy blue rug in the middle of the floor. I am on the couch, looking at her. She has one leg raised and I focus on the bend of her knee, the way the lower thigh meets the upper calf. I wonder if the crevice is moist.

"I'm bored," she tells the ceiling in her unidentified accent. I have repeatedly asked her where she is from but she only looks downward and says she doesn't want to talk about it.

"We could always . . ." I begin but she cuts me off with a sharp look.

"I'm all sexed out. Besides, it's too hot."

"We could turn on the air conditioning."

"I'd still be sexed out."

"Okay."

She lets out a loud breath, an alien version of 'I'm bored,' and spreads her arms out to either side—crucified by boredom.

"Or . . ." she begins. "We could give you a haircut."

This takes me by surprise. My hair is not overly long but, eager to please her, I rub my hand through my locks and say, "Yeah, I guess it is getting kind of shaggy."

"Very shaggy," she says.

"Well then . . . let's give me a haircut." And for the first time in what feels like hours we both move. I slide off the couch and she languidly stands, breaking up the crevice created by her knee-bending. I resist the urge to touch my fingers to that area. "Where do you wanna do this?"

"How about the kitchen?"

"We can't do it in the kitchen. I'll think about hair in my food every time I eat."

"But you don't cook."

"Regardless. No. Not in the kitchen."

"The bathroom?"

"The bathroom would be just fine."

We go into the bathroom and I sit down backwards on the toilet. She dislodges the mirror from the wall behind the sink, its suction cup popping, and puts it on the back of the toilet. Sliding open a drawer in the vanity she pulls out a pair of black-handled scissors, clipping the air a couple of times to get the feel of them. The sound makes me think of someone waving a sword in the air. I do not like looking at myself in the mirror so I close my eyes, figuring the hair is going to start falling soon enough anyway.

She leans against me, resting her hips against my shoulderblades, and says, "So, how do you want it?"

"I'm not picky," I say. "Just something different is fine."

"Okay. Keep your eyes closed until I'm finished. I want it to be a surprise."

"I was planning on doing that anyway."

Then she starts cutting. I have no idea of what it looks like or even how much hair she is taking off. Still seeing my face frozen there in the mirror behind my closed eyes, I try and imagine myself with a variety of different hairstyles. Hopefully she doesn't make me look silly. She gets really into the haircut. Maybe she has found her calling or something. She is humming a tune I can't identify. Probably some kind of song from her unidentified country. She blows on the back of my neck to get the hair off, never swiping with her hand. I find the tickling sensation erotic. I find the whole experience erotic. Me, sitting there defenseless before her while she yields her blades of steel above my head, her hips brushing against my back, the light humming, the gentle pressure of her fingertips as she bends my head this way and that. And the gentle gusts of her hot breath as she molds me into the type of man she wants to see.

"You can open your eyes now," she says.

Any arousal I may have felt dissipates completely.

"I look ridiculous," I say.

"I think you look like a rock star."

I run my fingers through it, thinking maybe if I muss it a little, it will look better, but it only makes it look more atrocious.

"No offense but this is the most hideous haircut I've ever had."

"Maybe *you* think so but it looks *fantastic.* You'll see."

"I don't know."

"Trust me."

"I think I need to take a shower," I say. "I need to get all this hair off my neck."

"Mmmm. Good idea. I'm going to go."

"You're welcome to join me."

"No. I think I'd better go."

I want to ask her where it is she is going to go because, really, I have no idea. She leaves my little apartment every day but I have never been to hers. I don't even know if she has one. I've never asked. I've always just assumed she had a place to live.

"Are you coming back tomorrow?"

"Of course," she says. "We'll celebrate your new haircut."

I don't know what to say to that. I try to smile and tell her I look forward to it.

I go to work the next day. I typically make it a habit to avoid looking in mirrors (the unkempt look is in) and have forgotten all about my haircut from the previous day. I work in a basement office with one other person, my boss, Mr. Gravity. He will not tell me his first name. At work there is a vestibule that promises something greater on the inside but it is just that, a vestibule, a little sitting area with a couple of chairs and a small table with some outdated gardening magazines littering it. When you go through the inside door the hallway goes no further. To the right is my office, my boss' office—we share. It is really quite uncomfortable. The office contains only one desk and we sit opposite each other on most days. Sometimes he pulls out his laptop, plopping it down on the desk and I have virtually no room to work at all. At those times, I have to scoot my seat back from the table and do my paperwork on my lap.

My job is really quite simple. I work in trash collecting. Not for the city or anything like that. People call the office when they have stuff the city will not take or stuff they do no want the city to take. Then, either I or Mr. Gravity answers the phone. One of us then places a call to one of our collectors. They collect said items and remove them to an undisclosed location. They then mail an itemized list of what was found in the person's trash and we compile a list of the net worth. I have yet to find a point to this job other than the paycheck.

Mr. Gravity is usually hostile. He is a balding man with an outrageously large mustache who does not know how to speak in a soft voice. Not that he hardly ever talks to me. Usually I only have to endure his voice when he is on the phone, which is quite a bit.

Today, when I get to the office, Mr. Gravity is waiting for me.

"Do you like my new sweater?" he shouts as I open the door.

His sweater is covered in the necks and heads of giraffes floating in a lawn green background. It is atrocious but I say, "Yeah, that's really nice."

But he has fallen silent, looking at my hair. His shoulders slump and he moves away from me as if he is afraid. Only then do I remember my ridiculous haircut. We go into the office and he immediately sets up his laptop. I have absolutely nothing to do so I kind of slink down in my chair where he can't see me over his computer screen and close my eyes for a few minutes of rest.

I am startled awake when he shouts, "I'm gonna take me a little nap!" and slides onto the floor under the table.

Now I don't even have a place to comfortably stretch my legs. I decide he is probably going to be out for a few minutes so I sneak out the door to smoke a cigarette. I'm still out there smoking when he comes out to fire me.

He doesn't launch into anything comforting or designed to cover himself in case of some kind of discrimination suit. He just says, "Go away and don't come back!" And then he clarifies that by saying, "It's because of your hair. I've thought about it and I just don't like it. I don't even want to be in the same room with it."

I don't know what to say. I don't know if there's anything I can say. After all, he's probably right.

"Get your stuff and go home," he says.

"I didn't bring anything. I don't have any stuff."

"Then just go home."

I do what he says, tossing my cigarette butt off into the alley, feeling his eyes bore into my back.

Why had I even trusted Jacinda enough to let her give me a haircut? It's not like we have known each other that long. I don't even know where she was born but I am pretty sure she knows just about everything there is to know about me. I never trust anyone with my hair. I guess it is easy to second guess myself, walking down the alley after being fired because of that haircut. If I had been promoted, I probably wouldn't think anything of it.

It isn't until my bus ride home that the haircut's power reaches a mythical proportion.

There are two people on the bus when I first get on. At first I think this is odd. I am so used to getting on during the afterwork rush it takes me a moment to remember it is before noon and I have just been fired.

The bus makes another stop and a girl gets on. She can't be any older than a teenager. She looks like she spends a whole lot of time at the mall. Not bad looking but not my type at all. Out of all the seats on the bus, she chooses to sit down right next to me, smiling and popping her gum. I find gum chewing to be a loathsome sport and think it should be banned. She looks at me and smiles something vaguely predatory.

Digging in her purse, she comes up with a cigarette. No one smokes on the bus. It is completely forbidden and has been for a number of years so, at first, I think maybe she is just a smoker who needs to cradle a cigarette in her fingers or something to dull the craving. But this is not the case. She blazes up right there, blowing smoke out over the empty expanse of the bus. Second hand smoke is much more repellant than actually smoking. I look toward the bus driver's mirror, hoping to make eye contact with him, hoping he will notice this girl smoking on his bus. But he is oblivious, leaning over the wheel like a buffalo.

I think it's the combination of smoking and gum chewing that is really getting on my nerves. Why can't she just choose one? "I don't think you're allowed to smoke here," I say.

"Balls to that," she says, snapping her gum and taking a puff of her cigarette. "I'll do what I want. I'd like to do you."

"Excuse me," I say, thinking I've misheard her.

"You heard me. I said I'd like to do you. Right here in this seat." Then she moves her right hand, the one not holding the cigarette, across the seat, allowing it to rest on my crotch.

The idea is so off-the-wall as to be tempting but she isn't my type and I will not be able to live with myself if I ever allow myself to be seduced by someone like her. And there is Jacinda. I couldn't cheat on her.

The girl leans over and runs her gummy, smoky tongue over my ear.

"Hey," I say, trying to push her away.

But she is persistent, practically on her knees. She is grabbing my hands and putting them all over her generously proportioned body but I only feel more repulsed.

"I can't help it," she says. "I think it's the hair. You look like a singer or something."

That does it. I can't take it anymore. I shove her from the seat. She goes sprawling into the floor across the aisle. Her skirt pulls up and I notice she is wearing red-striped underwear, like a candy cane. I rush up to the front of the bus. The bus driver, apparently sensing my desire to leave, brakes the bus and opens the door. I rush out of the bus without looking back.

What the hell is going on? I wonder.

I don't even know what part of town I'm in. This probably isn't good. It doesn't look like a very good area. I decide to just start walking and avoid any alleyways or abandoned buildings that look like they might be home to gangs.

After nearly an hour of walking, I reach an area I am vaguely familiar with although it is still a good distance from my apartment. I wonder why the bus driver was even out this direction. It doesn't even seem like he was going in the general direction of the apartment. Unless I got turned around somewhere along the way, which was a very distinct possibility. I've never been very good with directions. Or maybe the same bus didn't always follow the same route. Maybe the route was different before noon than it was during rush hour. Whatever. There isn't any point in thinking about it now.

It is early afternoon and I figure I probably have about another hour of walking to do. My feet hurt and I just want to be home, resting on my couch. I wonder if Jacinda is going to be there. I have the revelation that I have to break up with her. At first, I pretend not to know where this notion comes from but it doesn't take me long to think about it before I realize I know exactly where it comes from. That girl on the bus. That hideous girl on the bus. She liked my hair. She liked it a lot. She was overcome by it. It was enough to make her want to have sex with a complete stranger on the bus. She said it made me look like a singer. Singer, rock star, I figure it's really all the same. So, somewhere in my mind, I equate that girl with Jacinda and this somehow taints Jacinda. I know I can never look at her in the same way. Not to mention that she is the one who gave me this haircut. She can, to a certain extent, be held entirely responsible for today's events.

As I am thinking these thoughts, something else occurs.

I am attacked.

It's not as bad as it sounds, really. It is just an old woman but she is clearly crazy, brandishing a cane. I have always found something sinister about canes like, at any moment, the bearer of the cane could reach out and slap me across the head. This crazy old woman does just that.

"Heathen! Whoremonger!" she shouts.

I can't even fathom why she thinks her outdated words are insults but I am unnerved nonetheless. She moves fast for an old woman. Almost supernaturally fast. I take off running but I have to go a good two blocks before I am out of her cane's reach. My back is burning with the swats. I think she caught me on the side of the knee with one of the blows.

On the good side, this run speeds up my arrival at the apartment. Once I have lost the screaming old lady for good, the apartment is only a block away. I get to the door, panting and out of breath, and use my key to get into the communal foyer before walking up the stairs and thinking about how tired and rubbery my legs feel.

When I open the door to the apartment, a comforting breakfast smell greets me. Jacinda stands in the kitchen, spatula in hand, and says, "Eggs. A whole lot of em."

The kitchen table is covered in scrambled eggs, heaped up, yellow and steaming.

"That *is* a whole lot of eggs," I say.

"You bet," she says. "Nothing is too much for my man."

I cringe at the thought. Never did I think that phrase would come from Jacinda's mouth. I see a weakness there I never saw before and I don't like it. It only reaffirms my thoughts about what I have to do.

"Why are you sweaty and out of breath?" she asks.

"You wouldn't believe it," I say only, secretly, I think she really would understand.

"Hmmm," she says. She looks confused for just a second or two, like she was going to say something but forgot what it was, and then says, "Eggs."

"I've got to do something about this hair," I say.

"Oh no you don't," she says.

"I have to. I can't live like this."

Knowing she is going to try and stop me, I charge toward the bathroom, shutting and locking the door once inside. With the door locked, I feel safe. I feel like I can do exactly what I want to do. I look in the mirror just to make sure the haircut hasn't grown on me. Of course it hasn't. It is ridiculous. Absurd. It just isn't me. No. That's not right. I know that's not right. Maybe it is *too* me. Certainly, I am ridiculous and absurd, not to mention a million other unflattering things. Well, that may be the case, but the hair still has to go. Having never been good with the scissors before, I pull my battery-powered clippers from the vanity drawer. Previously I have only used these to trim my sideburns but now I am going to take the hair down to the scalp. I am terrified of the shape of my skull but I can't keep this ridiculous farce on my scalp any longer.

There is a wettish plopping sound, repeating continually against the door. I imagine Jacinda is outside, throwing scrambled eggs at the door. I want to tell her to stop but know that won't do any good. She will do it until I have to leave the bathroom to go out and make her stop. Which is exactly what she wants. But I am not leaving the bathroom until the work is done. I slide the switch of the clippers to the ON position. The sound is somewhat satisfying, like summer insects, and the job only takes a couple of minutes.

Now finished, I don't like the result but it is better than what was on it before.

I open the door, wondering how Jacinda will react to my latest haircut.

Wading through scrambled eggs, I find her in the kitchen curled into a ball. She looks up at me with something like hate.

"No," she says. "I can never love you with that haircut."

As soon as she says this I realize I don't want to break up with her. The thought of her leaving makes me want her to stay more than anything. I want to uncover her mysteries. Find out who she really is. Standing there, not a strand of hair on my head, I feel naked and exposed, like she can see right into my brain.

"It'll grow out," I say. "It's just hair."

"No. I can't . . ." she stands up, tears running down her cheeks. She reaches the front door and casts a sad look back in my direction, letting her hand flutter in something like a wave.

I wander over to the couch and sit down, waiting for my hair to grow.

THE DRIVER'S GUIDE TO HITTING PEDESTRIANS

ONE

The pedestrians are out of control. They travel in packs. Snarling, hooting, ing, legs like tree trunks.

TWO

The drivers are lonely. I am a driver. I am lonely as fuck. No wife. No children. No home. I have sacrificed everything for Sunset 6, my van.

THREE

My van is so named because of the six airbrushed sunsets emblazoned on it. The red blood of pedestrians, drying to a dark brown, looks good mixed with the various hues of orange and yellow. I used to wash the blood off every night before going to park in the alley. Then there were other drivers, more pedestrians, something involving the internet and government subsidies. Ritualistic vehicular manslaughter became a game, complete with cash prizes. Evidence became a trophy. And while everyone was far from cool with it, the opposed were in the minority. Boring, passive little shits.

FOUR

It goes like this. Every time a driver hits a pedestrian, he or she earns points. It's very simple. A pedestrian is only safe when he or she is in his or her house or car. Not all pedestrians are pedestrians all the time. However, because everyone who owns a smart phone is always in the system, the more time a pedestrian spends walking, the more his or her value increases. In other words, the more points a driver gets for hitting them. All drivers get points for hitting pedestrians, but you can tell the really serious drivers. We're the ones with custom vans, our identities airbrushed or enameled on the side of our vehicles. The most serious of us rarely even leave our vehicles. The pedestrians with the highest point values are usually in rural areas or metropolitan areas. Rural pedestrians simply have to walk farther to get to things and most of them have land to walk around on. Some metropolitan pedestrians don't even own cars, so they walk all the time, really racking up the points. I tend to stick to the cities because the volume is greater. I can usually take out four or five pedestrians a day.

Okay, so "take out" is a little strong. I usually just hit them. The goal is not to kill them, although that does happen at times. To kill a pedestrian ends in a point deduction. After hitting them, it's up to the driver to get them to a hospital. Our country is greatly underfunded. Ambulances are rare. Fortunately, because our country is more or less run by insurance companies, hospitals thrive and the game is great for business. Death is cheap compared to a near fatal impact.

FIVE

So here's the situation. Each month is a different round. It's currently June. Round 6. The round ends at the end of the month, both a pedestrian and a driver winner are declared, and the cash prize is paid out. I have yet to win, although I keep getting better. I'm currently in third place. It's the final day of the round. I'm in Dayton, Ohio, home of the pedestrian leader, Omar Hidalgo. I figure I either need to hit ten regular pedestrians today or one Omar Hidalgo. Dayton is not a huge city, so Hidalgo shouldn't be impossible to find. There are other pedestrians to hit and there's a hospital right on the edge of town. Meaning that, after each hit, I won't have to spend an inordinate amount of time shuttling the victims back and forth. That's a pain in the ass and another strike against a rural pedestrian hunt.

But the pedestrians here are even more savage and out of control than the pedestrians across the rest of the country.

SIX

I'm squatting down in the back of Sunset 6 shitting in my man-size litter box when the first wave of pedestrians hit. They slam into the van, come at the tires with sharp objects, attempting to disable it. They could be acting on their own or they could be working for Kathy Coffee or Frank Unicorn. Kathy Coffee's currently in first place. She drives some kind of delivery truck with a steaming cup of coffee painted on the side. The steam from the coffee spells out the word "KILL." I've never met her but she seems like a badass. Frank Unicorn holds second. He has a purple van with teardrop windows and a ferocious unicorn, equipped with an abnormally large penis, airbrushed on the side. It's my opinion that Unicorn has cheated his way to the top. Mostly by paying off feral pedestrians to take out his competition. Whatever he's paying them would be a drop in the bucket compared to his cash prize if he actually manages to win. It's a risk. It's a gamble. But it's strictly against the rules to make physical contact with the other drivers. To do so is instant disqualification.

I hope to make sure he loses.

I crank open the back window of the van and shout, "Get away, you little fuckers!" hoping they'll think I'm threatening. Hoping they won't realize I'm squatting down, my pants around my ankles, my ass hanging over a box of cat litter.

Surprisingly, they run off. One of them shouts, "That's for the Unicorn!"

I'll fuck them up if I ever see them. They don't know what Sunset 6 is capable of.

SEVEN

After thoroughly Windexing my ass and giving it a quick wipe, I grab my phone to see where things stand. I'm still in third place, but only by a pedestrian. Hidalgo is still on the loose. Unicorn is in Dayton as well, which is just what I thought given the gang he sent to rough up Sunset. Coffee is in New York. That could be bad. She could hit pedestrians all day long in New York. But there's a lot of congestion there, meaning she will spend a lot of time stuck in traffic. But she has a ten pedestrian lead on me and a nine pedestrian lead over Unicorn. There are, however, several superstar pedestrians in New York. If she hits one of them, there is no winning.

And while I'm checking these stats, Unicorn has managed to take down two peds. A twofer. Rare and powerful.

I need to get moving.

I hop out of the van to give it a quick survey. To see how many tires the peds managed to take out.

It's only one.

I can change that in no time.

EIGHT

I change the tire and hop back in the van. Nothing's changed. I have a considerable lead over fourth place and with this being the last day, everyone else has probably given up. Luckily it's a Wednesday so people have to go to work. Otherwise the peds would just stay in.

I fire up the van, slam it into gear, and roar out of the alleyway, anxious for some kind of satisfying contact.

NINE

I turn the music up really loud. The van vibrates all around me, an obnoxious and protective lover. Something that is wholly mine. I scan the sidewalks looking for prey. I barrel through intersections and take turns on two wheels. I speed through 25 mph neighborhoods at 70 or 80. I run a hand through my greasy hair, sip my coffee that I roast in the van and brew over the heat of the engine, make and consume a sandwich from fixings I keep in a cooler between the seats, check my phone repeatedly, and think it would be cool if I had someone to talk to.

What will I do if I win?

Buy some fucking friends.

TEN

Hidalgo might be staying in today. But he's a superstar ped. He needs the challenge just like we need the challenge. Probably for the same reason Coffee hasn't hit anyone all day. They're both toying with us. Meaning Hidalgo is probably looking for me as much as I'm looking for him.

Unless he's looking for Unicorn.

ELEVEN

Unicorn hits his third of the day and it isn't even noon yet. He'll be at the hospital shortly. Hidalgo might be there too.

I head for the hospital.

On the way, I roar through an intersection at Wayne and Wilmington. In my rearview mirror, I see a man cautiously step out into the crosswalk. I slam on the brakes and punch it into reverse. Anticipating his possible retreat, I turn the wheel slightly and hit him straight on. He drops out of sight so I miss his impact with the ground and the subsequent roll. The possible blood spray. I log the hit in my phone and get out. I throw open the back doors. The ped is crumpled on the street. It's possible his hip and maybe an arm are broken. He might be in shock. I check to make sure he has a pulse and when I feel it thudding faintly in the side of his neck, I hoist him up and toss him into the back of the van.

He's trying to talk to me. Saying pitiful things like he's in a lot of pain and I busted him up real good. As we get closer to the hospital he becomes more abusive, telling me he hopes it's worth it, that he really hopes I win since he'll never be the same again.

There are a lot of things I want to say to him but I don't. I just say, "Don't die," and turn the music up louder to blot his pathetic voice.

TWELVE

I pull up to the hospital entrance. Because I've already logged it into my phone, there are two nurses waiting with a wheelchair. They can't get the ped out of the van fast enough. I'm opening the back doors and I think I'm yelling at them but I can't even hear myself over the music pouring out of Sunset so the whole thing is just a furious blur. I hop back into the driver's seat and quickly turn around.

Unicorn passes the intersecting street right in front of me. He must notice me too. He stops and backs up, right in front of me. Goading me.

And I notice his van has two additions and something inside me breaks.

I turn the music down and then off.

I sit in the cab of Sunset and even the sounds of the city around me fade away.

It's just me, the gentle idling of Sunset, and my anger.

THIRTEEN

I wasn't always a serious driver. I used to be a sometime pedestrian and sometime driver just like almost everyone else. I was married and had a wife and a house and all that. My wife's name was Peggy. She died. Hit by another driver while she was in her car. An honest accident. Something that almost never happens now.

Her face was now painted on the airbrushed unicorn's ass.

That was the first addition I noticed.

FOURTEEN

The second addition was Hidalgo. He was on top of Unicorn's van. He looked at me and made a jerking off motion before slapping himself back down onto the roof, probably securing himself with spikes driven into the steel.

It was, in a way, the safest place for him to be. Since he was untouchable in his place as the pedestrian leader, he didn't necessarily need to spend the day out walking. He could play. He could goad and chide just like Unicorn was doing. Unicorn couldn't hit him if he was on top of his van. And for me to hit him would mean hitting Unicorn as well.

Unicorn peels out and I follow him.

FIFTEEN

My blood is up. This is the end game. Something has to happen and I'm trying to work something out in my head. I grab a handful of coffee beans and pop them into my mouth, crunching and swallowing them. I wash it all down with some moonshine I keep in the glove compartment. I strip off my shirt. I want to wear the blood of Hidalgo. And, perhaps, once the game is over, I'll want to wear the blood of Unicorn as well. There is absolutely no game law stating I can't beat him to a bloody pulp in a bar fight.

Unicorn speeds onto Route 4 heading west and out of Dayton.

I feel drunk and boastful.

I don't have any friends but I have a few living family members scattered throughout the globe. I systematically punch their speed dial coordinates into my phone—it doesn't even matter which one I'm talking to—and shout ridiculous things at them. I ask them if they're watching this shit then say of course they are, everyone is. I tell them I drive to win and I'm going to win everything. I'm going to win the moon and space and existence. I feel blood coursing through my body and pounding in my head. It feels like all of my hair is standing on end. I tell them I am an electric man here to drive lightning bolts into the faces of my enemies.

I slam my phone onto the center console so hard it almost breaks.

Back on with the music. Up loud.

Down with the accelerator, keeping a safe distance from Unicorn so he doesn't slam on his brakes and force me to hit him. To come all this way and be disqualified would be like suicide. Losing to Unicorn would be like snorting a pile of my broken teeth.

SIXTEEN

We're barreling down the state route and it's gray and humid and threatening rain and I think this might be a good thing. It might loosen Hidalgo's grip. The rain will sting his face and his eyes. If he comes off that van, I'm nailing him. Hopefully not hard enough to kill him.

Unicorn comes to a screeching halt and I almost plow into the back of him. He's disabled his brake lights. Hidalgo slides forward, in front of Unicorn's window now, but he maintains a grip on the spikes. Unicorn backs up and slams on the brakes. Speeds forward and slams on the brakes. This continues several more times. I'm not sure what I have to do other than stay out of the way. I check my phone. Coffee still hasn't hit anyone. Then again, the more Unicorn and I dick around, the greater her chances of winning.

The more Unicorn goes back and forth, the less likely it looks that he's going to loose Hidalgo from his handholds. I need to think of something else to do. Maybe drive back to Dayton and see if I can find one of those packs. Maybe take out five or six peds at a time.

But being this close to Hidalgo is maddening.

Unicorn being this close to Hidalgo is maddening.

Peggy's face on that unicorn's ass is maddening.

SEVENTEEN

I pull alongside Unicorn. He goes backward. I creep forward and stop. He speeds forward, probably not even thinking, and slams into the back of Sunset. And like that, he's disqualified. I'm in second now. Hidalgo goes sliding over the top of my van and onto the road in front of me. I punch the accelerator but it takes Sunset a second to leap forward and Hidalgo is already out of the road.

He has to be hurt. I don't see any sign of him.

Until I look in my rearview mirror.

He's leaping into the passenger side of Unicorn's van and Unicorn is then driving around me, steam billowing up from his hood.

I'm not really sure what just happened.

I check my phone and find out that Unicorn is indeed disqualified.

Coffee still hasn't hit a ped.

The smartest thing to do would be to drive back to Dayton and hit as many pedestrians as I can.

But Hidalgo is right there in front of me.

I just need for him to get out of Unicorn's van. I'm not sure this will happen. Most of our vans are well equipped and capable of keeping the driver comfortable for at least a week. Why the camaraderie between Hidalgo and Unicorn? Doesn't Unicorn harbor some kind of resentment toward Hidalgo? If it hadn't been for him clinging to the roof of his van, he might have stood a good chance of winning.

Unless he knows something I don't.

EIGHTEEN

Unicorn continues to drive along Route 4, down past Germantown. The steam continues to billow. He's losing speed. He pulls into a gravel pit. His truck idles in front of the unnaturally blue quarry lake, the airbrushed unicorn with Peggy's face on the ass trembling with the dying rhythm.

I again turn my radio off.

Unicorn and Hidalgo are just sitting in the cab of the van, staring at me. Maybe daring me. But to do what I don't know. We are now in a fairly rural area. For some reason, there is no one working at the quarry and everything is silent except for the occasional car up on the state route.

I check my phone.

Coffee still hasn't hit anyone else.

I'm so close to Hidalgo.

All he has to do is step out of the van.

I'm prepared to wait until midnight.

NINETEEN

The moonshine has made me kind of tired so I keep chomping coffee beans. I want to get out of the van so I can brew some fresh coffee over the heat of the engine but I know Hidalgo will take that chance to run. If he even plans on it. Occasionally, I open my door and feign stepping out, hoping this will coax Hidalgo out. At one point I unleash a vicious rant in their direction. They do not pay it any mind.

Around dusk, Unicorn steps out of his van and says to me, "This is your time to shine, isn't it, Sunset?"

I would drive into him but then I would have to waste time taking him to the hospital, going in the opposite direction of Hidalgo.

Unicorn has a can of spraypaint in his hand and he crosses to the side of my van. He begins spraypainting something on the side of it. I try to see what it is from the side mirror but I can only make out the first letter. It's an "L".

While the mystery of what he's spraypainting and the desire to beat him to a pulp are overwhelming, I remind myself I need to keep my eye on the prize.

Hidalgo.

A life of fortune.

A lonely life of fortune.

But with money, people would gravitate toward me. I could keep them entertained while entertaining myself. I could buy a huge house and have parties every night and . . .

I realize I don't like any of that stuff.

I don't like parties.

I don't like people.

I don't like party people.

I liked being a mechanic. I liked coming home to Peggy and reading about races in other countries. I liked to dream of going there. I liked the dream. I didn't know if I would like going there or not. Definitely not alone.

Coffee still hasn't hit a single pedestrian all day.

There hasn't been a single update since Unicorn's disqualification.

I think about bribing Hidalgo to come out and let me hit him. Just a tap. But that's against the rules and with Unicorn right there, I'd never get away with it.

It gets dark. The summer night air is alive with the smell of honeysuckle and the burning rubber and exhaust from the state route. In the distance, in the dark and silent woods, someone has started a fire. Insects hum and rattle their drawn out rhythm.

This is how they're going to beat me.

If Hidalgo survives, he gets a fairly large sum of money too. It's possible he's worked out something with Unicorn. It's possible that's what they've been talking about in the cab all this time. In low tones so I can't hear. It's possible even that they've both worked out something with Coffee. Two winners split three ways is still a pretty good bank.

And like that, all hope leaves me. This van was customized on hope and now it's empty.

I've been empty for a long time. Maybe I just confused hope with self-delusion.

I look into Unicorn's van and see his and Hidalgo's faces lit by the orange light of the dash.

I turn the radio up, the sound roaring out into the night.

I reverse until I'm a fairly good distance away. Then I slam the van into drive and shoot forward.

There isn't an explosion or anything. Just the satisfying impact and crumple of metal on metal. The concussive shattering of glass. The cold slurp of the water in the gravel pit.

And we're all wrapped in metal and broken glass and water.

And we're all going down into the cold depth of the gravel pit.

All going down.

All together.

THE
SEX BEAST
OF
SCURVY ISLAND

ONE

At the sound of the doorbell, Brock Rockhard stopped in mid-thrust. The girl below him, the one they currently called Project 26, opened her eyes wide and stifled a moan.

"It's okay," Carrie Godown called from the next room. "It's just Sheriff Dent."

Brock continued thrusting.

Project 26's moans continued.

The camera ran.

TWO

Carrie opened the front door. "Sheriff Dent."

The plump officer stared over her shoulder, trying to find the source of the ecstatic moaning.

"You caught us in the middle of filming."

"I could come back."

"You're welcome to watch." Carrie knew Dent was only into gay animal porn but felt like she should offer anyway.

"I think I'll pass this time."

"What brings you by?"

"I have a favor to ask."

"Come on in."

Carrie retreated across the living room of the old farmhouse to the doorway of the back bedroom, pausing momentarily to look at the rippling muscles of Brock's deeply tanned back and the scabby knees of Project 26. Zeke Loner stood in the corner of the room, recording everything.

"Make sure you get the angles right," she told him. "Most guys don't want to stare at Brock's ass for ten minutes."

He flipped her off. She slammed the door.

She turned back around to see Dent staring at Frump, the dog with perfectly formed male human genitalia, lying on his back and sleeping. Dent's eyes glazed over. He absently rubbed himself through his uniform pants.

"Sheriff?"

He blinked and shook his head. "I think I zoned out. Where was I?"

"You had a favor to ask."

Carrie sat down on the couch in the middle of the room, shoving the napping Emma Inside over. Emma opened her eyes and stretched. Carrie told her to go make some coffee.

Carrie stared at Dent's blooming erection. "Sit?"

"Maybe I should."

Sadly, she knew the cause of Dent's erection was the poor sleeping dog and not her perfect figure, experimental black hair, and multitudinous piercings.

Dent sat down and stared dreamily into space.

"Your favor?"

"Oh, right." He took his hat off and placed it over his crotch. "I've got this old friend who's a sheriff down at a place called Scurvy Island."

"I've heard of it."

"You have?"

"Yes. I hear they have some wonderful. . . local sights."

"And that's the problem, I'm afraid."

"The local sights?"

"All those delicious girls and boys. It seems like most of the young women are pregnant and the young men are getting killed in ridiculous ways."

"Ridiculous how?"

"They had to dig one of them out of a cow's stomach."

"Oh. Did the cow swallow him?"

"They believe he was inserted into the cow's rectum. The Sheriff—his name's Denny Rogers—is pretty baffled. As you know, that's a tourist area and most of the tourists come for the services of the young men and women. A lot of people have stopped coming. Sure, they've had their share of fetishists, and the women and remaining men are still willing to work, but soon Scurvy Island as we know it is just going to dry up."

Frump roused himself from the floor and trotted toward the sound of Dent's voice.

"And you want us to . . ."

Dent held out his hand and rubbed Frump's head.

"Find out who's doing all the raping and killing and put a stop to it." He scratched vigorously below Frump's chin. "Yeah, that's a good boy."

Carrie looked on in disgust. "Why doesn't the Sheriff do that?"

"To be honest, he's not very smart. And he might be a little corrupt. I think the Grassville Gang can do better. We'll make it up to you financially, of course. And you'll have free room and board while you're down there."

Frump latched onto Dent's leg and began thrusting against it.

"If it's okay with the others, then we'll do it."

Carrie stood up. She could tell she had already lost Dent. His eyes were rolled back in his head as Frump continued to thrust and pant against his leg.

"I'll leave you two alone." She stood up and walked toward the kitchen to check on Emma. As she reached the door, she heard Dent cry out in ecstasy.

"That's twenty dollars," she called over her shoulder.

"On the table," he called back before shutting the door on his way out.

THREE

Carrie leaned against the counter. "What a dirty pig."

Emma poured her a cup of coffee. "Dent?"

"Yeah."

"He's all right. Just different."

"So what do you think about going to Scurvy Island?"

Emma let out a resigned sigh. She'd just come off a three-day Guzzle bender and felt deflated.

"Not to film. To work."

Emma looked down at the floor, her blond hair falling over her shoulders.

"I *do* like to solve crime," she said. "Almost as much as I like to fuck."

"I'll go tell the boys."

"Are we bringing . . .?"

"Project 26?"

"We're going to have to give her a name eventually."

"When it's time. Maybe we'll just leave her here to keep an eye on Frump."

"You think that's a good idea?"

"It's either here or back to the truck stop glory hole."

FOUR

Before traveling, the Grassville Gang liked to drink copious amounts of Guzzle Blue to keep them alert.

Together, they charged out of the house shouting, "Grassville Gang to the rescue! Grassville Gang forever!"

Brock Rockhard with his red bandana, sunglasses, cut-off denim shorts, and nothing else save his flip-flops and grossly unhealthy tan.

Carrie Godown with her black dreadlocks and piercings, black tank top, black gypsy skirt, black-framed glasses, and black combat boots.

Zeke Loner with his messy hair, dark brown sweater, khaki corduroys, and whatever his book of the day was.

And Emma Inside, the once reluctant virgin, now sex-starved and ready for action with her long straight blond hair, form hugging white t-shirt, and skintight jeans worn low around the waist.

Together, they charged for the deep purple van. The driver's side of the van featured an airbrushed depiction of two kids in wheelchairs playing badminton.

The girls slid open the side door and hopped in.

The boys jumped in front.

Brock turned the key in the ignition.

Loud music blared.

Brock turned to shout at everyone in his dumb guy party voice: "It's a good thing this baby can *flyyyy!*"

And he hit the accelerator, taxiing onto the runway cut through the middle of a cornfield and, as the van went faster and faster, as they were almost out of runway, Brock flashed a thumbs up to Zeke, who opened the glove compartment and pulled the super special lever. The van lifted and took to the skies.

Excited, as they always were before a job, hopped up on Guzzle, the girls disrobed and began going at each other.

Emma feverishly and continuously moaned, "Ow, my pussy's sore."

Brock watched them in the rearview mirror, pulling his cock out and massaging himself. Carrie was covered in tattoos of the ugliest people she had ever seen. She added new ones all the time. Brock found their hideous faces, made even more hideous through Carrie's contortions, quite erotic.

Zeke opened up Camus' *The Stranger* and began to read.

They reached Scurvy Island in no time at all.

FIVE

Zeke wasn't sure why Brock always flew the van. Maybe he'd been a pilot at one point but, whatever shred of intelligence he'd once had had long since been obliterated by copious amounts of varied Guzzle products.

They circled the island until they found what could have been a runway.

"Landing!" Brock took his hand off his penis to guide the wheel.

They came down rough, in an explosion of vaginal juices, lubricant, sweat, come, and curses.

The girls threw open the sliding door and exited the van, pulling on clothes and adjusting them, buttoning buttons.

Zeke got out and calmly slid his old paperback into his pocket.

Brock got out, slammed the door violently, and sniffed the air for blood or vagina.

The front driver's side wheel was bent under the frame.

"You trashed it," Carrie said.

"I'll fix it!" Brock shouted. He slammed his head into the quarter panel above the tire and rocked the van over on two wheels. Grabbing the tire, he gave it a yank. It came off in his hands. Brock was extreme. In fact, two years ago, he'd changed his name to Brock X-treme. Zeke wasn't sure what kind of Guzzle he'd been on at the time but it didn't last long and ended with Brock going to jail, followed by rehab.

"Now you *really* trashed it," Carrie said.

Brock hurled the tire. It came down a few feet away and rolled a while before coming to rest in the sand. Then he collapsed next to the van, pulled his knees into his chest and started breathing heavily.

"It's o*kay*," Emma said. "Just calm down. I'm sure somebody here can fix it."

"I think that's the Sheriff." Zeke pointed across the hood of the van.

A deeply tanned man with shoulder length gray hair and a well-clipped beard approached them. He looked a lot like Kenny Rogers before the botched plastic surgery. He wore long khaki cargo shorts, ratty white Converse, and a stained white wife beater with SHERIFF written across the ample stomach in black marker.

"Denny Rogers?" Carrie stuck out her hand. She hoped the Sheriff wouldn't notice it smelling like vagina.

"The one and only."

"We hear you have a problem," Carrie said.

"That I do. You here to help me out?"

"Well, we're always up for a good mystery. We like solving crime. Almost as much as we like to fuck."

Rogers looked momentarily perplexed. "I think there's been too much fucking round here, if you ask me."

"Tell us all about it."

"Tell you? Hell, I can *show* you."

SIX

They hopped into the Sheriff's car, a rusted-out hulk that would fit about a hundred people, and drove to a barn toward the middle of the island. They didn't pass a single car. Didn't see a single person out walking. The entire island felt abandoned.

Standing in front of the barn doors, Rogers said, "I wasn't really sure what to do with them so I just put em in here."

He swung open the doors and entered the barn. The Grassville Gang followed him in.

There must have been a hundred or more stalls. A pregnant woman was in each one. They were all naked, holding their huge stomachs and looking sadly at the Gang, as though they had come to free them.

"I'm runnin out of room," Rogers said. "And the tourists are runnin out of entertainment. Therefore, I'm runnin out of tourists and runnin out of money."

"Why are they in stalls?" Carrie asked. "It doesn't seem right to just lock them up like that."

"I have to go," Zeke said. He had his book out, holding it in front of his crotch. Carrie wondered if he was appalled by the conditions or really needed to read. He *couldn't* have been aroused.

"I think we've all seen enough," Carrie said.

Brock had moved up to one of the stalls and begun massaging a woman's breasts.

"Mmm," the woman moaned. "I'm lactating too. . . You want summa that? Huh? You want summa momma's milk?"

Brock took a step back and the woman began shooting milk through the air.

"Sick!" Brock shouted and ran out of the barn in fear. Everyone else followed.

SEVEN

They hopped back into Rogers' cruiser and drove through the quaint island town until they reached a pizza shop. Once inside the pizza shop, they were the only ones there besides the young island boy behind the counter.

They slid into a booth and Brock barked, "Five large pies!"

"Sir," the island boy said quietly. "You're going to have to put on a shirt."

"It's okay," Rogers said. "He's with me."

"But the health code . . ."

"I have one hundred and twenty-six pregnant women locked in a barn. Fuck the goddamn health code."

"Whatever . . ." The boy retreated back behind the counter.

"Can we get some beer?" Rogers asked.

"A keg!" Brock shouted.

The boy wheeled out a keg and sat five plastic mugs on the table before struggling to hoist the keg up. The boy filled the glasses. Beer was actually, technically, now Guzzle Gold, but most people still just called it beer. The boy again disappeared.

Rogers took a long sip of his beer and shook his head. "I know you guys probably think it's inhumane to keep all them girls locked up like that but I have reason to believe that . . . when they deliver the babies, they might be dangerous."

"How do you figure?" Emma asked.

"I personally examined each one of them."

"You mean like their pussies?" Brock said. He held his left hand into a circle and punched his right index finger in and out of the hole.

"Yes." Rogers looked embarrassed. "That's exactly what I mean."

Brock nodded his head up and down knowingly and made a raunchy face.

"Now hold up. I didn't fuck any of them. I just examined them. Anyway, they each demonstrated similar signs."

"Similar signs?" Carrie asked.

"The person who impregnated them had a very large penis."

Carrie wondered if it was larger than Zeke's.

"Have you come to any conclusions?"

"I think the same person impregnated all of them over a three-day period. Of course, that's been months ago. I wasn't even aware of the problem until recently and I'm afraid it might be too late."

"It's not too late," Carrie said. "We'll find him. Whatever it takes."

The island boy came back and covered the table in pizzas. Everyone was ravenous and busied themselves eating. By the time they were finished, Rogers and Brock were both too drunk to carry on a conversation. Carrie, Emma, and Zeke helped them out to the car and Zeke drove to the Labrador Hotel. They left Rogers in the car and went into the hotel to confer.

EIGHT

The Grassville Gang did their best thinking while shooting porn.

Once inside their hideously dilapidated room, they flopped Brock onto the bed. Emma turned on the docked iPod and tuned it to some mood music. The mood music was one long repetitive piece Zeke's friend recorded using his keyboard under the moniker Your Mom's Face. Carrie opened up the cooler and passed around bottles of Guzzle Pink. Zeke stood behind the camera.

Carrie unbuttoned Brock's denim shorts and pulled them down his legs. Everyone in the Grassville Gang was natural except for Brock, who was a mess of chemical tanning, electrolysis, implants, steroids, and numerous penis modifications. No one was sure where the penile parts came from but it was so racially diverse it was the genital equivalent of a college brochure.

Carrie began sucking his scarred, multi-colored member and Emma forced some Guzzle into his mouth.

"Wait," Zeke said. "What do we call this one? We can't just start shooting without a title."

"Hmm?" Carrie mumbled around Brock's penis.

"A title?"

"Oh." Carrie came up and held Brock in her hand. "Why don't we just call it *Out of Their Heads (And Clothes) Part 12?*"

"Sounds good."

"Thanks." Carrie went back to sucking Brock.

Emma stood up, downed her Guzzle, and slowly took off her clothes while making eye contact with the camera. She finished off the Guzzle and tossed the bottle into the corner where it shattered.

"Mmm, I'm so wasted," she said into the camera. "And my pussy's sore."

She stumbled getting up onto the bed and straddled Brock's face. He was out of it but still knew enough to perform his duties. His tongue began lapping at Emma's pink vagina.

"Ow, my pussy's so sore."

Carrie stopped fellating Brock and began removing her clothes. The more flesh she revealed, the more disgusting tattoos Zeke had to focus on. Her latest addition, just above her left breast, looked like a man who had a horn growing out of his cheek. She left her glasses on.

"You like this one?" She stroked the new ugly man. "I want that horn up my wet cunt."

She slipped off her white underwear and flicked her clitoral ring. She downed the rest of her Guzzle in one gulp. She staggered and took a step backward. Zeke zoomed in on her unfocused eyes.

"Fuck," she said. "I wanna fuck till I puke. Yeah? Does that sound good? You wanna make me puke?"

Then she was on the bed, straddling Brock's wildly erect cock. "Oh, yeah," she said. "Bury that shit in me. Oh fuck. I'm gonna rip off my nipples."

She tugged vigorously at her nipples.

Zeke set the camera up on the tripod and checked to make sure it was focused on the bed.

"Ow, my pussy's sore," Emma cried.

Zeke took his clothes off behind the camera. He was thin, pale, and hairy. His penis hung down to his knees.

"You gonna gag me with that thing?" Carrie said. "Huh? You gonna slide that monkey arm down my throat till I puke? Puke and come?"

"Yes," Zeke spoke in an enunciated monotone. "Whatever. Life is meaningless. Might as well fuck until we die."

He approached the bed. While riding Brock hard, Carrie grabbed Zeke's cock and slowly took it all into her mouth, down her throat.

"Ow, my pussy's sore."

The bass from the stereo had kicked in and the Grassville Gang was lost in the haze of Guzzle and sex.

Carrie gagged and pulled away from Zeke's monster cock. "Aw, fuck, baby. You gonna shoot your jibbles on my teeth?"

"No." Zeke sounded bored. "I just want to (*sigh*) stick this big cock in your tight hole."

"Get your jibbles off? Aw, fuck! I wish you could fuck my spine. Oh, baby, yeah. I'm gonna roll on the floor."

Carrie pulled herself off Brock and began rolling on the floor. She rolled until she hit the wall and then rolled back until she hit the bed. Zeke went to the head of the bed and bent Emma over Brock. She eagerly started sucking Brock, proffering her ass to Zeke. "Careful," she said. "My pussy's sore."

"The pain will make you feel more alive."

Zeke slapped her ass hard and mechanically.

"Hurdle!" Carrie stood up from the floor and took a running leap over the flesh heap on the bed. She flew into a table and broke it. Covered in blood and splinters, she stumbled over to the bed and started smacking Emma in the face as Emma sucked Brock, Zeke pounding her from behind.

"Stick your fingers in that asshole!" Carrie shouted savagely.

Zeke obeyed, plugging Emma's ass with his middle finger.

Things became even hazier after that. The foursome ran through every combination possible until they reached their grand finale.

"Matter spatter!" Carrie shouted.

"God. Pussy's so fucking sore . . ." Emma hissed through gritted teeth.

Carrie lay down on her back. Zeke and Emma rolled Brock on top of her. Emma fed his cock into Carrie's vagina. Carrie shouted, "Shitstorm fiasco!" Emma sandwiched her hips between Brock and Carrie's heads so Carrie was lapping at her cunt and Brock was tonguing her asshole.

Zeke lubed up his penis and worked it into Brock's filthy rectum. This was a special scene. They could only do this when Brock was really, really wasted. Zeke worked away for a few minutes and Carrie shouted, "Matter spatter!" again.

Zeke pulled out, kneeled beside Brock and began slapping his back with his feces-covered cock.

Emma crawled up to the head of the bed, splayed her legs, and put a bag of ice on her vagina before sticking her thumb in her mouth, looking into the camera, and crying.

"Get your jibbles out!" Carrie yelled. "Get em all in that shit!"

"Yes. I'm getting ready to come in this shit. This shit I got from fucking another man in the ass."

"Oh God. Oh fuck! I'm gonna fucking puke. Puke and bleed and pass out!"

Just as Zeke was ready to come, the power went out.

"What?" he said.

He heard things moving around. Brock wasn't under him anymore.

Carrie kept shouting, "What the fuck is going on!"

"Ow, my pussy's sore? Even though I have ice on it?" Emma called. Zeke wasn't sure where she was.

Then he heard a shrill voice coming from somewhere near the window.

"Ha ha! You may be almost as good at solving crime as you are at fucking, Grassville Gang, but you'll never catch The Impregnator!"

And then the window shattered and all the power came back on.

"Zeke?" Carrie called from the bathroom. "You'd better come here."

Zeke walked into the bathroom, his bare feet crunching across the debris.

"I'm going to be sick," Carrie said.

The bathroom was covered in shit, blood, and entrails. Brock lay in a pool of gore in the bathtub. Carrie vomited into the toilet.

Emma came into the bathroom and said, "I think that guy raped me. My pussy's sore, like, for real this time."

NINE

"Okay," Zeke said. "We need to call Sheriff Rogers."

"I gotta get out of this bathroom." Emma turned back into the main room.

"And we should probably all put some clothes on," Zeke said.

He grabbed his clothes from the floor and put them on. He grabbed his cell phone from his pants pocket and called Rogers. It rang and rang.

"He's not answering."

"Did you call 911?" Carrie was now examining herself in the mirror and pulling splinters out of her skin.

"Do you think that even works here?"

"Sure. Why not? It works everywhere."

Zeke shrugged and dialed 911. It rang and rang.

"I'll go down to the lobby," Emma said. "See if they can help us."

"Don't tell them about Brock," Carrie warned.

"Who?"

"The lobby people. We don't want to incite panic or anything."

"Whatever."

Emma left the room and walked down the tiled hallway until she reached the front desk. A rotund islander sat sleeping in his chair, head lolling back, drool slicking his chin.

"Sir?"

She noticed something off to her right, outside.

"Yeah . . . just a minute." The clerk wiped the drool from his chin and picked some crust from the corners of his eyes.

"Never mind."

"Thanks for waking me up then."

"Fuck you."

"Fuck *you.*"

"Good comeback."

"Fuck your face."

Emma rolled her eyes.

Through the glass doors of the lobby, Emma had spotted Rogers' car, exactly where they had left it. She walked out into the humid night. Rogers was asleep in the front seat. Emma could hear his phone ringing. The windows were open. She wondered how the residents and tourists felt safe. She reached through the window and grabbed the phone.

"Hello," she said.

"I'd like to report an emergency."

"Zeke?"

"Yeah. Emma? Where are you?"

"Right out front. Our beloved and faithful sheriff is passed out in his car."

"Well get him up here."

TEN

Rogers surveyed the crime scene from the doorway. He said he didn't want to get any closer. He already felt queasy.

"Looks like he's the victim of a rapid enema machine."

"A what?" Zeke asked.

"A rapid enema machine. It's a machine that gives enemas in rapid succession. If it's turned up too high, it'll suck the bowels right out."

"I've never heard of one of those. Why would someone *need* one of those?"

"Well, it's theoretical, but that's what it looks like."

"So you just made that up?"

"I theorized it. We need to get that body out of here."

"We?"

"Yeah. Well, you guys. I'll hurl if I come anywhere near it."

"Aren't you going to call an ambulance? An EMT? A coroner?"

"Dead. Dead. And dead."

"Shit."

"I *told* you I have a fuckin crisis on my hands."

"Fine. What do we need to do?"

"We need to get it down to the car and then we'll throw it in the ocean. That's the island way."

"Sounds like that's the lazy way. Don't you need it for evidence or something?"

"If we see a person with a rapid enema machine, I'll assume we have our man."

ELEVEN

They rolled Brock's body into a tarp and loaded it into the trunk of the car. Zeke wondered why working with the Sheriff felt an awful lot like working with a serial killer.

Once at the beach, they rolled Brock's body into the water, but the tide kept bringing it back. Zeke was suddenly emotional.

"Let's go back to the car and hit some Guzzle Green," the Sheriff proposed.

The others followed, Zeke wiping away tears.

Once at the car, Rogers uncapped a bottle of Guzzle and took a swig before passing it to Emma, who did the same.

"Now," Rogers said, "you said this thing raped you?"

Emma nodded her head. "I'm pretty sure. My pussy feels sore. Almost raw."

"But you didn't get a look at him?"

"It was so dark."

"I think it's obvious what we need to do."

The bottle had made its way back to Rogers and he took another healthy swig. The others stared at him, awaiting his answer.

"We need to gather up all the remaining men on the island and you need to have sex with them."

"That's . . . retarded," Zeke said.

"We'll make them all sign releases. You can film it."

"Now it's starting to sound profitable. Emma? Are you up for that?"

"My pussy's really sore but. . . if it'll help crack the case of The Impregnator, I'm up for anything."

"Great." Rogers clapped his hands together. "We'll want to get started right away. Naturally, you'll have to fuck *me.*"

"Can you get this?" Zeke pulled the camera from the backseat of the car and handed it to Carrie.

"Why? What are you doing?"

"Looking for clues."

Zeke hopped into the car and pulled away, watching Rogers stroke his comically small penis in the rearview mirror.

TWELVE

Zeke was terrible with directions and spent two hours driving around the island before he finally found the barn. An erection strained against his corduroys as he pulled to a stop. He walked to the barn doors and realized they were padlocked. If he were Brock, he would have just ripped the wooden doors off the barn. Thinking about Brock made him sad. He went back to the car and pulled the keys from the ignition. There were several keys on the ring. Hopefully, one of them would open the barn.

Zeke paused and made sure he really wanted to go through with this. Maybe this was the only way he *could* go through with it—in the name of research. Clue hunting.

He had never been with a pregnant woman before. It was something he had always fantasized about. When he was young, his mother was pregnant all the time. She had to have children so she could sell them for food. Zeke's mom and dad thought it was much easier to stay home and fuck and then sell their children than going out to get a real job. Zeke had always thought the pregnant form of a woman was how they were supposed to look.

Now was his chance. A pregnant woman. An absence of cameras. The acquisition of knowledge. It didn't get a lot more exciting for Zeke.

He unlocked the lock and pulled the door open.

The smell that greeted him was not pleasant.

He was sort of hoping they could do it in front of the other pregnant women, but Zeke didn't think he'd be able to put up with that stench.

Over the years, he'd learned that women enjoy sex as much as men. And if you have 126 women in a room, the chances were good that at least one of them wouldn't care who it was she fucked.

He unbuttoned his pants and pulled his colossal cock out. It was fully erect and stood out at a right angle from his body.

"Who wants it?!"

Luckily, there was a woman close by so he didn't have to wander back into the stench of the barn. He let her out of the stall and took her back to the car. What followed was brutal, satisfying, and highly informative.

THIRTEEN

Fucking in the high noon sun had exhausted Emma. Nineteen guys later, she chugged a bottle of Guzzle Clear and threw herself into the ocean to get the sweat and come off her body. Her vagina was beyond sore. While she didn't mind all the sex, she wished they had found a suspect.

She had her suspicions about Rogers, but it had absolutely nothing to do with the length or girth of his penis.

On the beach, Carrie stripped off her clothes and waded out to Emma.

"Any luck?" Carrie asked.

"None." Emma stuck out her bottom lip.

"Who would do something like this?"

"I don't know. There doesn't seem to be a lot of people here."

"*Why* would someone do something like this? I guess that should be the first question."

Emma splashed at the warm, clear water. "Money?"

"But if their money's in tourism and you impregnate or kill the whores who bring the tourists . . . That just doesn't seem logical."

"Maybe someone wants to turn the island into a baby factory."

"That practice is still frowned upon by the mainstream."

"Maybe we should just match the DNA from the fetuses."

"You think this place has a lab or anybody who'd know how to do it?"

"Maybe it's a spite crime."

"Like revenge?"

"Could be."

"Look." Carrie pointed farther up on the beach. Rogers appeared to be arguing with a bald man in a black suit. "Who's that?"

"That was guy number six."

"Oh, right. I didn't recognize him with the suit."

The men continued to argue, pointing back toward the town and the middle of the island. Things became more animated and the large man in the suit punched Rogers in the stomach, doubling him over.

Emma headed for the shore on rubbery legs. "We need to help."

Carrie reluctantly followed her.

By the time they made it up to the beach, the man had already left. Rogers was collapsed on the sand, dramatically holding his head and kicking his legs.

Carrie noticed a strange deformity on his right arm and couldn't help asking him about it. "What's wrong with your arm?" It looked like he was missing an elbow.

"Jesus, think you could help me up?"

Emma helped him up while Carrie continued to study the odd depression on his arm.

"So you gonna tell me or not?"

"That." He pointed to it, spitting sand from his mouth. "I was born without an elbow, that's all."

"That's stupid. I've never heard of that."

Emma placed a consoling hand on Rogers' shoulder. "Who was that man?"

"That guy . . . Oh, just an old friend."

"You know," Carrie said, "if we're looking for suspects, you shouldn't keep things secret from us."

"It was Dean Mahoney. He's not a suspect. Is he, Emma?"

"Definitely not." She held her index and forefinger two inches apart.

"So who is he?"

"He's just a guy I owe money too, all right?"

"Maybe he's working with The Impregnator."

"The only person Mahoney works for is Mahoney."

Carrie started to say something else when Zeke pulled up in the car, cutting her off.

"I think I have a clue!" Zeke called from the car. He opened the door and stepped out, holding something up in the air.

"What the hell is *that?*" Emma cried.

"It's a fetus!" Zeke smiled for the first time Emma could remember.

FOURTEEN

"Ew, what does a fetus have to do with anything?" Emma asked.

Zeke must have been hitting some sort of Guzzle on the way back. Or maybe he was just excited. He hopped back and forth, holding the fetus around one ankle and waggling it in front of Rogers and the girls.

"Is it still alive?" Carrie asked. "Maybe you shouldn't be handling it like that."

"No. It's okay. I had to snap its neck."

"Zeke!" Emma cried.

"No, it's okay, Em. It isn't human."

"Looks human."

"No. It's not. It's a demon baby. I had to kill it because it kept trying to eat my heart. See? See?" He held the fetus' head in his left hand and pulled back its upper lip. Perfectly formed teeth grew from the gums. Most of them were pointed. Then he poked its navel. "See? See here? No umbilical cord or anything. It just fucking crawled out!"

"Out of the pussy?" Emma asked.

"I think it's called a womb," Carrie said.

"But it still has to come through the pussy."

"It's actually a vagina."

"Whatever. You're a fucking prude. I still don't think Zeke should have killed it."

Rogers stood behind the girls, chewing on his thumb. He looked nervous or maybe nauseated.

"But if it had been a full-grown demon trying to eat *your* heart out, it would have been okay, right?" Zeke goaded.

"Well . . ."

"So I was just being proactive."

"And this is your big clue?" Carrie asked. "You were in the barn with all the pregnant women, weren't you?"

"I actually took one woman into the car. The barn smelled foul. I don't think they have any bathrooms in there. And they might have lactation wars when they get bored. Anyway, I've always heard that one of the best ways to induce labor was through sex."

"There are other ways," Carrie said.

"Look, we all have needs, okay? Anyway, I almost lost my penis as a result." Zeke dropped the fetus to the ground. "Look at it." He pulled his pants down and brandished his huge cock.

"My god!" Emma cried.

It was raw and gnawed-looking.

"I hope it heals," Carrie said. "I hope it was worth it."

"Regardless, I think we need to have a conference."

Emma said, "It just won't be the same without Brock."

"I could stand in," Rogers said.

"I think we need to be alone," Carrie said.

Rogers looked dejected.

"We could use the girl," Zeke said, pointing to the lifeless-looking woman in the back seat. "They're all kind of hypnotized or drugged or something. Maybe we can shock her into remembering something."

"Maybe," Carrie said. "Sheriff? Can we get a ride back to the hotel?"

FIFTEEN

They piled into the car and headed back toward town. Emma gathered up the fetus and held it on her lap like a real baby. Zeke made out with the new girl.

"She's gamey," Carrie said. "She's going to have to shower before the conference."

"You're just jealous," Zeke said.

"Yes. I wish I had a demon fetus growing in me."

Emma looked at the demon, horrified. "Do you think I have one of these in *me* now?"

"It's possible," Zeke said. "Once we get back, you'll have to go to the doctor. You don't want to carry something like that to term."

"Fuck!" Emma rolled down the window and started to throw the demon out but Carrie stopped her.

"We might need to examine it."

"Carrie's right," Zeke said before continuing to make out with the girl. She looked mostly comatose. Maybe that's what Zeke liked about her.

Carrie spotted Dean Mahoney walking on the sidewalk on the opposite side of the street, his back to them.

"Isn't that . . ." But before she could even get his name out, Rogers swerved the car and clipped Mahoney. The bumper hit his right knee, kicking his leg out from under him and sending him rolling off into the parking lot of an abandoned convenient store.

"Shit!" Emma said. "You just hit that guy, what's-his-face."

"Accidents will happen," Rogers said. "I wouldn't worry too much about it."

"But he could be hurt really bad."

"Next stop, Labrador Hotel!" Rogers was clearly changing the subject and refusing to talk about it.

Once at the hotel, they grabbed the demon and the woman and headed for the lobby doors. They were locked. A hand-lettered sign was taped to the door on the left. It read: CLOSED PERMNANTLY.

"That's no good," Emma said.

"Maybe we can confer in the car," Carrie said.

"I don't see any other choice," Zeke said.

Carrie said, "You're gonna have to leave Stinky out here."

"What about shock therapy? What about information? I think she needs to be part of the conference."

"Fine," Carrie said. "But there's no room for Rogers. Besides, he might be a suspect and we might have to talk about him."

They walked back to the car. Zeke asked Rogers if they could use his car to film *Doped Teen 3*. He said he didn't mind, got out of the car, and leaned against the hood. Zeke guessed they would just have to whisper if they needed to talk about him.

SIXTEEN

The conference was long and vigorous. Emma was sexed out and Zeke's penis was like raw hamburger so it took them forever to come. The other girl was unresponsive and kept dozing off or passing out. Her vagina was loose and bloody from delivering the demon. The demon lay on the dash the entire time. Rogers stood outside the car and played with himself through the pocket of his shorts while looking back over his shoulder and then pretending he hadn't been looking.

They were going to question the girl as soon as they finished but she drifted off and they were unable to wake her up.

Zeke checked her pulse.

"Dead," he said.

"Dead?" Emma asked.

"Dead," Zeke repeated.

"Who's dead?" Rogers asked.

"The girl. You're not supposed to be listening."

"We should call 911 again," Carrie said.

Zeke found his cell phone in the pile of clothes on the floorboard and punched in the digits.

Rogers' phone rang and he answered, "Scurvy Island emergency."

"Sheriff?"

"Yep."

"There's a dead girl in the car."

"I'm sorry to hear that."

"Shouldn't we call an ambulance?"

"Are you an idiot? Didn't I tell you everyone was dead?"

"What about you? Don't you know CPR or something? Surely law enforcement must learn some of that stuff. Even security guards learn that."

"I'll see what I can do."

Rogers came around to the rear passenger side of the car, opened the door, and dragged the girl out. He laid her on the ground and began fondling her.

The Grassville Gang, still naked, stood around him and looked down with disapproval.

"Are you even trying?" Zeke asked.

"Why don't you go take a walk or something," Rogers said. He continued looking down at the dead girl. He might have been crying. "I know you just want to talk about me anyway. You think maybe *I'm* this sex monster, this Impregnator . . . But you're wrong."

Carrie said, "I guess we should put our clothes back on."

Zeke said, "Don't have sex with the corpse, okay?"

Rogers shook his head. "I can't promise anything. Remember to take your dead demon baby with you."

SEVENTEEN

The remaining members of the Grassville Gang put on their clothes, grabbed their dead demon baby, and headed for the beach. Once at the beach, they walked along in the fading daylight, passing around a bottle of Guzzle Green. Carrie produced a dossier and began reading through it. She always had one of these. No one was really sure where it came from.

"Maybe we should sit down," she said.

They found a bench. Carrie and Zeke sat on the bench and Emma sat in the sand, facing them.

"So," Carrie began. "Nearly every male on the island is dead and nearly every female pregnant. We know the perpetrator is someone calling himself The Impregnator."

"And," Zeke raised a finger of proclamation, "he may not necessarily be human."

Carrie continued to flip through the dossier. "I would say with all the women getting pregnant within a few days of each other, he's not human at all."

"Or he's *super*human." Emma giggled. "Maybe we should hire him to be part of the Gang."

"This is serious, Em." Carrie kicked sand at her.

"One man was filled with helium. One man was beaten to death with a shoe. One man was sodomized to death with a chair. Grisly. One man drowned in his toilet. One man choked to death on an ice cream cone. One man . . ."

Zeke waved a hand. "We get the point."

"So why would someone do this?"

"It sounds like someone wants the island to himself."

"But who?"

"Sheriff Rogers comes to mind."

"But Emma had sex with both Rogers and The Impregnator and said they were nothing alike."

"I've been thinking," Emma said. "About my test. I don't know how accurate it is."

Carrie looked up from her dossier. "What do you mean? I thought your vag was a hundred percent accurate."

"It usually is. But it *was* dark when The Impregnator raped me. What if he was wearing some kind of prosthetic? Do you want to hear my theory?"

Zeke and Carrie both nodded their heads.

"I think this Impregnator character *does* have a prosthetic penis. And I think he's outfitted it with some kind of demon semen."

"Demon semen?" Carrie asked.

"Yes. Some chemically altered substance he's been shooting into the girls. How else could he get so many of them pregnant in such a short period of time?"

"And they would have to be ovulating within a few days of each other . . ." Carrie said.

"And none of them could be on birth control or anything . . ." Zeke said.

"Unless," Emma said. "The demon seed just needs a warm body and not necessarily a womb."

"That's a good point," Zeke said. "But then why wouldn't he have just used the men, too?"

"Who knows," Emma said.

"Maybe he *did* use the men. Did anyone check to see if they were pregnant?"

Zeke stood up quickly. "Let's go to the cemetery and dig up a body!"

Carrie pulled him back down to the bench. "They don't use cemeteries, remember? They just throw them in the ocean. That's the island way."

"Again," Zeke said. "Who could it be?"

Carrie stood up from the bench. "I think we need to find Rogers and ask him a few more questions."

The sun was now almost completely gone from the sky, sinking into the ocean and turning it a dazzling orange. Zeke thought it looked a lot like Hell.

He noticed the tide creeping in at an alarming rate.

On closer inspection, it wasn't the tide at all.

EIGHTEEN

"Demon babies!" Zeke shouted.

Carrie squinted her eyes.

Emma turned around.

"Oh, fuck!" Carrie shouted.

"Quick," Zeke said. "We need to get to the car and get out to the barn. These things were probably incubating in the corpses tossed out to sea."

"And we need to get into the van. Get the weapons out," Carrie said.

"You girls go get the car. I'll get the shit out of the van."

They stood in a circle, even though they didn't really have time, and put all their hands on top of one another. "Grassville Gang to the rescue. Grassville Gang forever!" And they brought their hands up into the air, the horde of demon babies only a few feet away.

Carrie and Emma began running toward town.

Zeke began running for the van, which was only a little way down the beach.

NINETEEN

The demon babies were not hard to outrun, even though they were able to chug along on their legs rather than crawl. Zeke made it to the van, panting and tired, with a few minutes to spare. Beside the driver's side of the van was an odd shape on the ground. Only, it wasn't really odd. Just out of place. For a brief moment, Zeke thought it was Brock.

Drawing closer, he saw that it *was* Brock.

Had he somehow still been alive?

Had he crawled back here to the van to try and fix it in his final moments of life? Even after his closest friends had thrown him into the ocean, watched him wash back up onto shore, and then left him for dead?

But now he was definitely dead.

Lying out in the sun all day had not done great things for him.

Zeke tried not to become emotional as he crouched down beside him and ran his fingertips along Brock's red bandana. There wasn't any time to be emotional.

"We'll miss you, buddy."

Zeke looked at the wheel of the van, hoping the tire would be there, hoping the van would be fixed.

But it wasn't.

He opened the doors at the back of the van. He crawled inside and frantically grabbed their weapons. He preferred a battle axe. There was something very traditional about it. Brock had used a flame thrower. Emma used a small chainsaw and Carrie used a garrote.

It was a lot to carry.

Turning to step out of the van, Zeke was confronted with three demon babies, hissing as their little hands clutched the shiny chrome bumper.

Zeke primed the flame thrower and strapped it onto his back. He pulled the trigger and flames burst from the barrel.

"This is for you, Brock!" Zeke thought that was something Brock would have said. He pulled the trigger again.

Then he leapt from the van, through the stench of fuel and burning baby demon flesh, and ran into the early dark.

TWENTY

As soon as they had taken off running, Emma had tossed the dead demon baby over her shoulder, hoping it would ward off more of the demons. They had run as hard as they could.

Now, halfway into town, Emma stopped.

She leaned against a palm tree and stuck her hand down her pants.

Carrie stopped and walked toward her. "Come on, Em. Now's not the time to rub one out."

"Ow, my pussy's sore. And it itches." She giggled. "And kind of tickles."

She pulled her hand out of her pants.

Carrie knew she couldn't have crab lice because she didn't have any pubic hair. She moved closer to see what Emma held between her thumb and forefinger.

"What is it?" Emma had her eyes closed, holding her hand as far as she could away from her body.

"It looks like a very tiny demon baby." Carrie took it from her. It was almost microscopic, but it was definitely a demon baby.

She threw it to the sidewalk and stomped it with her boot.

Looking back, she saw the demon horde approaching.

"We need to go. *Quickly.*"

They continued running back into town.

TWENTY-ONE

Zeke was not used to long distance running. Apparently, it used completely different muscles than lengthy and borderline supernatural sex.

Or maybe it was the extra weaponry he carried.

His vision blurred.

He knew the demon babies were behind him.

He tried to run back to where Rogers' car was parked in front of the Hotel Labrador, but was afraid his awful sense of direction would get him lost and in trouble.

Profuse amounts of sweat beaded on and rolled down his skin.

Was that a dune buggy in front of him?

It looked like it was in the middle of the street. An odd sight since they had hardly seen any cars on the road since arriving.

The dune buggy's lights flipped on. Bright. Blinding.

Zeke drew to a stop, his breathing ragged.

He heard the high whine of the dune buggy in front of him, the engine revving, the tires gripping the road and squealing toward him.

Behind him, the angry and hungry sounds of the demon horde.

Just as the dune buggy closed in on him, he dived to his right, rolling on the ground and pulling himself up quickly, readying his battle axe.

The dune buggy plowed through the demon horde.

Was someone here to help him?

Maybe he just didn't know the demon horde was there. It must have taken out four or five. They began crawling all over the dune buggy. Zeke still couldn't see the driver.

He wanted to run but, if the driver of the dune buggy had tried to help him, he didn't want to abandon him to the demon horde.

Ready to swing the battle axe, he approached the dune buggy.

The little demons were crawling all over the driver.

Maybe it was too late.

Then the driver stood up in the dune buggy.

He was huge. Heavily muscled. Red. Winged.

Zeke noticed the latter as he spread his arms, the baby demons lining them like birds come to roost.

Then Zeke noticed the huge appendage dangling between his legs.

This thing, Zeke thought. This thing is definitely not human.

Now that he didn't care about torching them all, Zeke fastened the battle axe to his belt and primed the flame thrower.

"Halt!" The Impregnator shouted at him. "The Grassville Gang stands no chance against The Impregnator and his minions. If you kill me . . . everyone dies."

Zeke wasn't sure what he was talking about. Wasn't everyone already dead? Maybe the women were still alive. But they were dazed, traumatized, possibly lobotomized.

Zeke shot a spray of flame toward the dune buggy and took off running in the direction he had originally intended. He ran off the road, zigzagging around palm trees, stands filled with employment guides and free newspapers, benches, and parking meters. If there was something that could potentially fuck a dune buggy up very badly, he ran around it.

The Impregnator followed him for a couple of blocks and then abruptly slammed on his brakes and headed in the opposite direction.

Zeke looked back over his shoulder to make sure there were no demon babies following him, slammed into a palm tree, and hit the ground with a clanging of weapons. He sat there for a few moments. The air was still. The humidity was intense.

In the distance, he heard the drone of the dune buggy and the high-pitched cackle of The Impregnator.

He needed to find the girls.

They needed to get to the barn.

He couldn't help but think something very bad was going to happen.

TWENTY-TWO

"Shit!"

"Fuck!"

"Where the fuck is he?" Carrie said.

Approaching the Hotel Labrador, there was no sign of Rogers' car.

"The shit skipped out," Carrie said.

"And left the girl behind," Emma said. The girl lay face down on the sidewalk.

"He didn't even have the decency to cover her up." Carrie shook her head in disgust.

"What a fucking goat's ass."

"What do we do now?"

"Zeke said something about meeting at the barn."

"No way." Carrie shook her head again. "There's no way I'm going there without my weapon."

"It's just a bunch of pregnant ladies."

"Are you crazy?! They're pregnant with demons! Demons, Emma! Are you so fucking oblivious you don't realize some really bad shit is going on here? Because if you don't, you seem to be the last one." Carrie swept her hands around her, motioning to the dark and hushed town.

Emma slapped Carrie hard, in the face.

Carrie punched Emma in the stomach.

It wasn't long before they were pulling at each other's hair and ripping clothes that would miraculously mend only moments later. Then they were on the sidewalk, tongues and fingers everywhere. Dildoes appeared out of nowhere. Five minutes later, the island shook with the crescendo of their simultaneous orgasms.

Rolling off one another, stickily, they stared dazedly into the night . . .

. . . and into a net dropping down over them. The net closed and they were lifted up and slung over the back of The Impregnator, thrown into the back of his dune buggy, and speeding away from the hotel.

TWENTY-THREE

When Zeke finally reached the Hotel Labrador, he was the only one there.

No girls.

No Rogers.

Just the girls' clothes.

He was exhausted. But he was also horny.

He picked up the girls' clothes, buried his face in their underwear.

He pulled his pants down and masturbated.

Then he went in search of a bike shop.

TWENTY-FOUR

Soon they were cruising through the dark night in the back of The Impregnator's gasoline-reeking dune buggy. There was another smell coming from The Impregnator. An awful smell. It smelled like death and old come and spoiled milk and maybe some shit, as well.

"You better let us out of here." Carrie struggled against the cargo netting.

"I'm afraid I can't do that," The Impregnator said. His voice was sinister. Was it electronically altered? It didn't sound like any type of voice either of the girls had heard before, save the abbreviated conference they'd had their first night here.

"I'll rip your cock off? And shove it down your throat?" Emma tried to threaten him but it came out in her porno voice and was entirely unconvincing.

"I'm afraid not. All I need to do is get you back to the barn and lure that other boy there. I have an especially ridiculous death planned for him. And as soon as he's gone, the island will be mine. ALL MINE!" The Impregnator laughed giddily.

"And what about us?" Carrie moved as close as possible to him, trying to hiss in his ear. It wasn't hard. The dune buggy wasn't very large. "You'll never impregnate us . . ."

The Impregnator laughed again. "But I already have." And he looked smarmily over his shoulder.

"We aborted Emma's," Carrie said.

"I gave you both another one. While I was carrying you to the buggy."

"My pussy *is* kind of sore," Emma said. "Again."

"*I told you,*" The Impregnator half-sang.

"You're forgetting one thing about the Grassville Gang," Carrie said.

"And what's that, darling?"

"We like to solve crime almost as much as we like to fuck."

"Liking and doing are two separate things." The Impregnator laughed and stomped the accelerator, throwing the girls back against the roll bars.

TWENTY-FIVE

Zeke found something even better than a bike. He found a pedal car. It had two big bicycle tires on back and a smaller tire up front. It had an orange flag on a stick attached to the back of it. The flag made Zeke think of golf. He hated golf. He tore the flag and the skinny pole off and threw them into the street. He stowed the weapons in the wire basket between the two back tires. He positioned himself in the pedal car. He was almost lying down. It took him a minute to get situated. Then, his eyes clouded with hate, he pedaled furiously, hoping he was traveling in the right direction.

TWENTY-SIX

The Impregnator and the girls reached the barn, the dune buggy skidding to a vicious halt.

The Impregnator lifted the net and suspended it from a nearby tree.

The demon baby horde surrounded the barn.

They parted for The Impregnator.

"Even if you get Zeke, Sheriff Rogers will stop you!" Emma shouted in a moment of desperation.

The Impregnator turned and approached the net. He batted savagely at it. "Don't you ever mention that name to me. That man is an unlanced anal wart. That man is a truckload of AIDS. That man is worthless . . . And you can rest assured that he's long gone."

"But he's the one who called us for help."

"After letting this go on for how long? He's too stupid to exist."

"He'll . . ."

"Shhh . . ." The Impregnator held a taloned finger up to his lips. "There are other things to do at the moment."

"But—"

The Impregnator struck the net again. "Please be quiet. Please? Can you do that? Or do you want me to feed your cunt to your friend?"

Emma was silent.

"Very good."

The Impregnator strolled back to the barn, flourishing his cape and switching his tail.

What had they gotten themselves into?

TWENTY-SEVEN

Zeke carried the girls' clothes in his lap. He knew they wouldn't have just gone off and left them. That meant The Impregnator probably had them. Zeke couldn't just go storming the barn. He would have to sneak.

Somewhere ahead of him, he heard the most awful sound.

Like a knight or an asshole, he followed.

TWENTY-EIGHT

"Witness the birthing!" The Impregnator cried out.

He threw open the barn doors and all the women came dazedly wandering out.

They were all nearly barking with screams.

The first one dropped to the ground and spread her legs. Emma wondered how she could have let her vagina get so hairy, how anyone could just let themselves go like that. She guessed if you were pregnant it just didn't matter.

The woman screamed and breathed rapidly.

Another woman dropped down next to her and began doing the same.

"The labor of multitudes!" The Impregnator shouted.

Carrie and Emma watched open-mouthed as the first woman's vagina ripped open in a shower of blood. A demon baby clawed his way out and crawled into the dirt.

"In only moments, my demon army will be complete."

"Not so fast, Impregnator!"

The girls heard the voice off to their right. As best they could, they turned in the net.

TWENTY-NINE

"Zeke!" they shouted in unison.

Zeke turned toward them and hurled his battle axe and their clothes. The axe sliced through the net and the girls landed on their feet, miraculously clothed, only a second later.

"Demons attack!" The Impregnator shouted. "I will not let you ruin my moment of triumph, Grassville Gang!"

One group of demons moved toward Zeke and another group moved toward the girls.

Zeke threw them their weapons.

They threw him his battle axe.

More women dropped to the ground. The Impregnator began seizing them, reaching up into their vaginas, and forcefully pulling the demon babies out, tossing them onto the dirt where they landed and scampered toward their prey.

Zeke spent too much time trying to prime the flame thrower. One of the demons clambered up his leg and tried to bite his neck. Not knowing what else to do, Zeke gnashed his teeth, taking a hunk of the baby demon flesh and accidentally swallowing it.

He brought the battle axe down on another one in front of him, splitting it in half.

He looked over at the girls. They were completely surrounded. The Impregnator was now forcing the pregnant women to the ground as they exited the barn, ripping the demons from between their legs. The night was alive with the screams of laboring women and the scent of their blood. Zeke didn't see any way out of this.

He started to feel weird.

Dizzy.

He dropped to his knees.

He kind of felt like vomiting but he fought to keep his gorge down.

It felt like he was spinning but he also felt . . . stronger.

A demon baby crouched at his ankle, sprang toward him, and latched on.

Zeke didn't feel a thing.

He picked the demon baby up and ripped it in half, saving a chunk to shove down his throat.

He turned to the girls.

"Emma! Carrie!" Even his voice was more powerful.

Emma finished sawing two of the demons' heads off at once. Carrie finished dragging the garrote through a neck and the girls turned toward him.

"You have to eat the babies! It'll make you stronger!"

Carrie garroted another one and drank from the geyser of blood shooting from its neck. Emma took off a tiny hand and popped it into her mouth.

In only a few seconds, they felt indestructible.

Now the Grassville Gang had the distinct feeling the tide had turned. They fought their way toward where The Impregnator crouched. They also ripped fetuses from the womb, ripped the babies in half, and took wild, random bites.

And just when they closed in on The Impregnator . . .

THIRTY

. . . he was nowhere to be seen.

In the distance, they heard his laughter. Around them, the demons' mothers were screaming and dying. The demon babies were all dismembered and either lay twitching on the ground or were in a state of retreat.

"What do we do?" Emma asked.

"We have to get The Impregnator," Carrie said.

Zeke nodded his affirmation.

The Grassville Gang loaded up in the dune buggy and shot back toward town.

Toward the Sheriff's office.

THIRTY-ONE

They reached the Sheriff's office to find Rogers' car haphazardly parked across the sidewalk. The front door was broken from its hinges. The window was shattered.

From inside the office, The Impregnator shouted, "You'll never stop me! You can never come between me and my life's work!"

Zeke approached the door and cautioned the girls. "Careful. It's slippery."

Once in the office, he flipped on the lights to reveal The Impregnator ensnared in a finely constructed prison of bondage cord, novelty handcuffs, dildoes, and fake vaginas.

Zeke approached cautiously.

"Who did this?" Carrie asked.

"You see," Zeke began, "when I found your clothes lying on the sidewalk, I naturally assumed The Impregnator had taken you prisoner. I quickly acted on our suspicions and assumed it had to be Sheriff Rogers. I knew he would have to come back to his office sooner or later so I broke into the Hotel Labrador and used whatever supplies I could find to construct this trap. He walks in the door, slides on the lubricant, and falls victim to the tensile strength of bondage rope and various latex products."

Zeke sauntered over to The Impregnator, placed his hand on the top of his head, clutched his mask and, yanking it away, said, "Girls, I give you Sheriff Rogers."

The face of Rogers was before all of them.

"I'm afraid you're not correct, Zeke," Emma said.

"What do you mean? That's Rogers."

"Yes. It is *a* Rogers. But this is the Sheriff's evil Siamese twin."

Zeke shook his head. "You must be joking."

"I'm afraid not." She approached The Impregnator and ripped away the sleeve of his left arm. "While The Impregnator was raping me, I noticed this unique deformity."

She pointed midway down his arm.

"A missing elbow!" they all shouted.

"That's right," Emma said. "Just like Sheriff Rogers. Only his was on the *other* arm."

"Where they were separated at birth!" Carrie said.

"Exactly. Sheriff Rogers had no reason to do these things but he did have a reason to wait so long to report them. He didn't want to sentence his only brother. Unfortunately, his brother was almost able to turn the complete island into his secret demon training ground and prepare for world domination!"

"And I would have gotten away with it too if it wasn't for you filthy pornographers."

"So Sheriff Rogers is innocent . . ."

"Well, not entirely," a voice said from the back of the office. Sheriff Rogers emerged. "This island's ruin is as much my fault as Lenny's . . . my brother's. I'd invested in everything until I practically owned the entire island. But I'm not good with money. I'm addicted to Guzzle and prostitutes and this is the wrong place for that. Eventually, I just couldn't make payments on my holdings. Everything fell into disrepair. The fewer tourists was a blessing at first. Things weren't so embarrassing . . ."

The Sheriff brought a hand up to his eyes and wiped the tears away.

"But you didn't do anything *wrong*," Carrie said. "You're just stupid."

The Sheriff nodded.

"So what now?" Emma said.

"Well," Zeke said. "I think we leave The Impregnator right here, get the hell off this island, and let the Feds sort it out."

"Only one thing left to do," Carrie said. She approached The Impregnator and pulled a blade from the waistband of her skirt. While Zeke braced The Impregnator's head, she carved a "G.G." into his forehead.

Reaching around behind The Impregnator, she pulled a canister from his back.

"*Nooo!*" The Impregnator howled. "Not my secret alchemical formula!"

"That must be the demon semen," Emma said.

There was a tube running down to the prosthetic penis outfitted in his costume. Carrie pulled the tube free and began spurting the semen on The Impregnator while he wept tears of humiliation.

THIRTY-TWO

It was dawn by the time they had finished. Stepping outside, the air had cooled considerably.

"Say," Sheriff Rogers said, "there really isn't too much here for me. Seeing as how you guys lost one, does that mean you have room for one more? I kind of like to solve crime. And I really like to fuck."

Carrie said, "Your penis isn't very large but, I guess if it's okay with everyone else, we could give you a trial run."

"You ever take it up the ass before?" Zeke asked.

The Sheriff didn't answer.

When they reached the van, they remembered it was damaged.

Zeke went around front to reinspect the axle.

"Hey!" he called to the others. "Look at this!"

The wheel was back on the van.

"How did this happen?" Zeke asked.

"I wasn't *just* hiding out from trouble," Rogers said.

"Welcome aboard," Carrie said. She and Emma slid the side doors open and crawled in.

Zeke was excited about finally being able to fly the van but, when he opened the door, Brock sat in the driver's seat.

Brock turned and said in a voice more powerful than he should have possessed, "Hope you're into necrophilia, buddy!"

Zeke, realizing he was into anything, climbed into the passenger side of the van.

Rogers climbed on top of him and began giving him a seductively hideous lap dance.

Brock powered the van down the street and bellowed, "It's a good thing this baby can *flyyy!*" in his dumb guy zombie voice.

And Zeke, he showed the Sheriff the super special lever.

Other Grindhouse Press Titles

#666__*Satanic Summer* by Andersen Prunty
#081__*The Next Time You See Me I'll Probably Be Dead* by C.V. Hunt
#080__*The Unseen* by Bryan Smith
#079__*The Late Night Horror Show* by Bryan Smith
#078__*Birth of a Monster* by A.S. Coomer
#077__*Invitation to Death* by Bryan Smith
#076__*Paradise Club* by Tim Meyer
#075__*Mage of the Hellmouth* by John Wayne Comunale
#074__*The Rotting Within* by Matt Kurtz
#073__*Go Down Hard* by Ali Seay
#072__*Girl of Prey* by Pete Risley
#071__*Gone to See the River Man* by Kristopher Triana
#070__*Horrorama* edited by C.V. Hunt
#069__*Depraved 4* by Bryan Smith
#068__*Worst Laid Plans: An Anthology of Vacation Horror* edited by
    Samantha Kolesnik
#067__*Deathtripping: Collected Horror Stories* by Andersen Prunty
#066__*Depraved* by Bryan Smith
#065__*Crazytimes* by Scott Cole
#064__*Blood Relations* by Kristopher Triana
#063__*The Perfectly Fine House* by Stephen Kozeniewski and
    Wile E. Young
#062__*Savage Mountain* by John Quick
#061__*Cocksucker* by Lucas Milliron
#060__*Luciferin* by J. Peter W.
#059__*The Fucking Zombie Apocalypse* by Bryan Smith
#058__*True Crime* by Samantha Kolesnik
#057__*The Cycle* by John Wayne Comunale
#056__*A Voice So Soft* by Patrick Lacey
#055__*Merciless* by Bryan Smith
#054__*The Long Shadows of October* by Kristopher Triana
#053__*House of Blood* by Bryan Smith
#052__*The Freakshow* by Bryan Smith
#051__*Dirty Rotten Hippies and Other Stories* by Bryan Smith
#050__*Rites of Extinction* by Matt Serafini
#049__*Saint Sadist* by Lucas Mangum
#048__*Neon Dies at Dawn* by Andersen Prunty
#047__*Halloween Fiend* by C.V. Hunt
#046__*Limbs: A Love Story* by Tim Meyer

www.ingramcontent.com/pod-product-compliance
Lightning Source LLC
Chambersburg PA
CBHW050801190726
48285CB00005B/1754

9 781941 918937